*The new Zebra Regency Romance logo that you see on the cover is a photograph of an actual regency "tuzzy-muzzy." The fashionable regency lady often wore a tuzzy-muzzy tied with a satin or velvet riband around her wrist to carry a fragrant nosegay. Usually made of gold or silver, tuzzy-muzzies varied in design from the elegantly simple to the exquisitely ornate. The Zebra Regency Romance tuzzy-muzzy is made of alabaster with a silver filigree*

D0995124

## A H

"Lord Waverly, I . . ." Selinda began, then stopped short. She had, for a fraction of a second, considered drawing off her gloves and fluttering her eyelashes. However, even Selinda knew there was hardly time to bring about a seduction. The place was all wrong, too, she supposed, for it was not even moonlit. She decided instead to rely on Lucy's recommendation to trust his Lordship; the only difficulty was in forming the proper words.

"Yes, Lady Selinda?"

"It's very odd, but my sister said I might . . ." Here she faltered again. However could she explain her peculiar reliance on the judgment of a mere child?

Waverly smiled encouragingly. "Miss Lucy is a great favorite of mine. You are fortunate to have her."

Although these unlooked-for words went a good way to reassuring her, Selinda's lower lip began to tremble. "I am afraid, Lord Waverly, that I do not have her at all. Oh! It has been the most horrid day!"

And even though Selinda had neither removed her gloves nor fluttered her eyelashes, Lord Waverly was suddenly moved to take her into his arms . . .

# A Sparkling Affair
## Mary Chase Comstock

**ZEBRA BOOKS**
**KENSINGTON PUBLISHING CORP.**

ZEBRA BOOKS

are published by

Kensington Publishing Corp.
475 Park Avenue South
New York, NY 10016

First Printing: May, 1993

Printed in the United States of America

# Chapter One

Lady Sybil Harroweby perched airily on the edge of a marble balustrade, a gauzy wrap draped carelessly over her lovely shoulders. From this vantage point she could easily view both the flirtatious couples gathered in the crowded ballroom, as well as their more passionate counterparts in the secluded pathways of the gardens below.

Both scenes were exceedingly diverting. Lady Sybil had always loved the feverish atmosphere of a ball and all the romantic entanglements, both public and private, that blossomed there. The fact that she had been dead for more than a century dampened her interest not at all.

Lady Sybil had haunted Harroweby House with characteristic good humor ever since her untimely murder in the frolicsome years after the dull and sanctimonious Puritans had been supplanted by the restoration of Charles II to his throne. With the return of Charles's festive court, London had suddenly become as thoroughly debauched as it had formerly been devout.

With more than sufficient time for reflection on her ghostly hands, Lady Sybil had thought more than once that she had, perhaps, thrown herself a little too energetically into the riotous spirit of the times. She could, perhaps, have practiced some restraint. She had been a rare beauty, though: a rose without a thorn, as a poet of her acquaintance had written; and if numerous bees had swarmed about her blossom, why, what was a helpless flower to do? Lady Sybil had blithely opted to enjoy their buzzing attentions.

Just who had murdered her, Lady Sybil did not know, nor, to be truthful, was she particularly interested. Between her husband's ambitious mistresses and her own host of jealous lovers, the number of likely suspects was embarrassingly large. Whoever was responsible, their poison had worked quickly and painlessly, and for this she was duly grateful.

What Lady Sybil had ascertained was that the spirits of the murdered were required by some vague set of spectral regulations to haunt the scene of their demise until they were reconciled to their fates and had forgiven the author of their departure. The gloomy spirit of Sir Henry Harroweby, a fourth cousin several generations removed, had explained it all to her one day when he took a break from rattling his chains on the attic stairway.

"It's all quite simple," he had told her. "As soon as you forgive your murderer and turn your thoughts to everlasting peace, you will be quite free to go.''

''Go where?'' she had asked.

''Why to your reward, of course,'' he answered irritably.

She looked at him blankly. Lady Sybil's religious training had been scandalously neglected.

''Heaven, you know. Angels, harps, solemn hymns. That sort of thing.''

Lady Sybil suppressed a shudder. The ghostly sphere had its drawbacks, of course, but thus far it certainly proved to be more interesting than celestial realms promised to be. ''I think I see,'' she said slowly. ''If I persist in condemning my murderer I stay here?''

''Yes,'' Sir Henry sighed heavily. ''I have very nearly overcome my own lack of charity. If my favorite nephew had not done me in, I would have been released some thirty years ago. However,'' he continued with a self-righteous sniff, ''family betrayals cut to the quick. Forgiveness comes slow indeed.''

''I doubt very much,'' she replied with measured calculation, ''that I shall ever forgive the villain (or villainess) or tampered with *my* tea. In fact, I vow I shan't.''

''Careful!'' Sir Henry hissed. ''You've just added ten years to your stay.''

''Never, never, never!'' Lady Sybil cried fervently as she envisioned angels, harps, and solemn hymns fading obediently into the distance.

''It's your future,'' Sir Henry had moaned with a gloomy shrug.

So Lady Sybil had entertained herself quite satisfactorily over the years, even though the family had abandoned the house for more cheerful settings for several decades. The escapades and affaires of the staff who maintained the residence were just as diverting as those of their betters. Lady Sybil not only observed, but often promoted, by various supernatural means, the romantic enterprises underway. Moreover, the house was now and then let to various families who wished to enjoy the London season, but had not purchased (or could not afford) their own establishment. Their presence allowed her to keep pace with the various *on-dits* of the social realm so dear to her heart.

For the most part, Lady Sybil's ghost was confined to the house and gardens, but early on she had discovered that if any item which had previously belonged to her were taken off the premises, she was free to follow it. Opportunities for excursions into Town had been limited, however, and one occasion in particular had taught her that it was best to remain where she was. In this instance, she had followed a footman entrusted with taking a small ormolu clock in for repair. She had anticipated only a brief outing, but, much to her dismay, found herself confined to the clockmaker's shop for two full weeks! Not only was the shop small and drab, but so was the clockmaker himself, and to make matters worse, his only romantic designs were on his own apprentice. Upon her grateful return, she was content to concentrate her curiosity on the denizens of Harroweby House.

8

*　　*　　*

Lady Sybil now turned her attention to the two gentlemen who sauntered onto her balcony: the Earl of Slaverington and the Marquess of Bastion, two of the most disreputable and perpetually impoverished rakes of the *ton*. Within thirty seconds of an introduction, they could, if the rumors she had overheard were correct, calculate the size of an heiress's fortune and the likelihood of their acquiring it by marriage or, failing that, lay odds on the chances of their deflowering the damsel. Their conversation, Lady Sybil determined with a knowing smile, should prove most informative.

"Damnably slim pickings tonight, eh, Bastion," Slaverington drawled. "If it weren't for the champagne, I'd have left an hour ago."

"Fine champagne," Bastion agreed with a resonant belch. "Any champagne is fine champagne. Seedy-looking crop of fillies, though. Not ten thousand pounds among'em, I'll warrant."

"All but that little Harroweby chit," Slaverington concurred, weaving slightly. "Where the deuce have they been hiding her these last months?"

Lady Sybil's attention was riveted. Harroweby? Why the girl must be some relation! She had realized in a vague sort of way that one set of tenants had been replaced by another in recent days, but she had paid no attention to their name. This was news indeed!

"Gets the whole estate when she's twenty," the earl went on. "Just look at that pack queuing up to claim their dances. A fellow can't get near her."

Lady Sybil peered into the ballroom. Her newfound relation was a pretty little thing indeed, blushing as she lowered her abundant eyelashes, soft brown ringlets stirring gently as she escaped for a moment behind her fluttering fan. The ghost sighed nostalgically. The child was also the very image of herself at that age. Not more than six months away from her governess, she decided.

"Yes, Lady Selinda Harroweby. A tempting little piece of baggage, if ever I saw one," Bastion leered speculatively. "Fortune, face and . . ."

". . . and a trio of suspicious Gorgons for chaperons," Slaverington finished glumly.

"That's that, of course. They might be got around, though, you know," Bastion mused speculatively.

"Not likely," his friend protested with an eloquent snort. "That oppressive aunt would skewer you with one look and serve you up on toast points. I wager twenty pounds you'll never get near the girl. Fifty that you'll never see her alone."

"No faith, Slaverington. It's the curse of our age. No faith at all. Make it a hundred," Bastion declared recklessly, downing his glass, "and I vow I'll either wed her or bed her."

"You don't have five pounds to your name, Bastion!" his comrade protested. "Let alone a hundred."

"But I shall in ten minutes. I see my cousin Waverly has just arrived."

"Ah, yes. The well-heeled Lord Waverly. You

are fortunate in your relations, Bastion, if not your wagers."

"The well-heeled, *eccentric* Lord Waverly," the marquess amended. "Were it not for the fact that I sometimes find myself under the hatches, I am afraid that even I would be tempted to avoid his company. Fortunately, I am one of his many good causes. Are we on, Slaverington?"

"For a hundred pounds? Why not, Bastion? I'm simply wasting for some good sport."

Had Lady Sybil been capable of real physical violence, the two libertines would by now have been nursing their wounds. She would have dearly loved to have seen the railing on which they were leaning give way and send them tumbling into the prickly embraces of the rose bushes below! As it was, however, she was forced to content herself with several violent (and thoroughly unladylike) curses which manifested themselves in an exceedingly chilly breeze. Fun was fun, she told herself, but family, after all, was decidedly family. Trifle with her descendant, would they? Not if she could help it!

# Chapter Two

Smiling charitably at yet another in a seemingly endless procession of seemingly identical young ladies to whom he was being introduced, Roland, Lord Waverly, silently congratulated himself on his unparalleled ability to suppress a yawn. Moreover, he had already survived the ball's first half-hour of tedium without either insulting anyone with his peculiar brand of wit or baffling them with his eccentric behavior. Such uncommon civility as this must certainly be tantamount to at least a year's worth of other magnanimous deeds.

Surely, he thought to himself, an unmarried man in possession of an admittedly staggering fortune could not be so rare a commodity as such onslaughts would make it appear. It was dashed annoying that the size of his fortune was so widely known, for it seemed his acquaintance, however unconventionally he lived his life, was as eagerly sought by hopeful mamas as were vouchers to Almack's. It would not have been so bad, he reflected, had any of the bevy he had met thus far been able to triumph over the mediocrity of manner with which society seemed so taken these days. Most decidedly they had not.

As he looked about him, he suddenly realized there were few among the gathering whom he recognized. That was hopeful, at any rate, he acknowledged a little cynically. Of late, his Lordship had adopted a new stratagem in determining which of his invitations to accept that would have shocked and annoyed all of his acquaintance: every few days he took the accumulated pile and tossed them into the air. Those which landed face up he accepted. Now that he came to think about it, he was not at all clear how he had come to receive an invitation to tonight's festivities, for he was certainly not acquainted with the family. How very odd, he mused with growing interest.

The young lady making her debut this evening was certainly one to capture his notice, though. "Diamond of the first water" was the hackneyed phrase that had immediately come to mind, but somehow it fell short. Yes, Lady Selinda Harroweby was beautiful and her manners engaging. By all accounts, she was excessively wealthy. She possessed an indefinable sweetness that was neither cloying nor missish, but there was something else about her, too, that his Lordship was unable to identify. Her favor was much sought after, of course, and Waverly been able to reserve a dance with her only by surreptitiously scratching off the name of another gentleman (who, he laid odds, would have bored her to tears) when she handed him her card, and inserting his own. It had been a long time since he had looked forward with quite so much anticipation to anything so patently conventional.

While he impatiently awaited his dance, though, Waverly made a game of dutifully mirroring the manners with which he was presented: he bowed, smiled, met proper observations with proper replies, and finally made his escape, but only after having resignedly committed his name to yet another young lady's dance card. His relief was short-lived, however, for he suddenly felt his hackles instinctively rise and, turning, found himself borne upon by his scapegrace cousin, the Marquess of Bastion. This unsavory person was closing in with alarming speed and determination.

"God grant me respite from family and friends," Waverly whispered to himself with pitiable exasperation. Then he shrugged. At least an attack of the sort he now anticipated was somewhat easier to confront than the feminine offensive with which he had been faced all evening.

"Roland, old fellow," the marquess began with the forced congeniality that customarily accompanied his perpetually impoverished state. "I must say you're looking in the very pink!"

"Just see my banker in the morning, Bastion," Waverly preempted him wearily. There was some minuscule entertainment, to be sure, in practicing polite rituals with hopeful misses, but hardly any whatsoever with annoying relations. "I've already authorized the advance."

The absurd look of shock mingled with chagrin that suffused Bastion's features was one of the few benefits Waverly was able to derive from this otherwise oppressive connection. He took a few moments to savor his cousin's gasping attempts at a reply. Indeed, he thought, the sleek marquess resembled nothing so much as a newly landed trout, floundering and gasping on the shore.

"Well, ahem," Bastion finally managed to sputter. "Er . . . Thank you, cousin."

"Ah, my dear cousin, as always, your eloquence is all the thanks I crave," Waverly replied with an elaborate bow as he turned to go. "Good evening."

"Half a moment, Roland," Bastion persisted desperately, grasping his cousin's sleeve. "Not to seem greedy, but, er, how much did you advance?"

"Greedy? Why of course not. Never entered my mind, old fellow. I thought perhaps two hundred pounds would be sufficient for now. One hundred for the debts I know about and another hundred for what you've likely incurred here tonight."

Waverly had to admit, albeit internally, that Bastion's attempt to control his astonishment was little short of spectacular. How in heaven's name did the fellow manage to bite his lower lip so hard without drawing blood? And why the devil was the fool always so flabbergasted to find that his requests were so easily anticipated? Waverly sighed inwardly and shook his head in polite consternation. Perhaps, he speculated, his cousin expended his meager mental gifts on the proper arrangement of his cravat. Hearing the music of the last set come to a close, he withdrew from his musings, and nodded to his cousin, "You must excuse me, Bastion. The guest of honor awaits me for the next dance."

"Lady Selinda!" the marquess exclaimed, his ordinarily slack features suddenly animated by a leer laden with blatant calculation. "What luck! You must introduce me, cousin. I fear I arrived too late to pass through the receiving line."

Waverly scrutinized his cousin with an exceedingly cold eye. "I *hardly* think so," he replied. "I've a reputation *of a sort* to consider, so forgive me if I have an eye to yours. I must say I am surprised to see you tonight in any case. I thought you were no longer received."

The marquess had, of course, wondered that very thing himself. It was quite true that he was no longer received in the best of homes anymore, and certainly not at coming out balls for innocent maidens. Although the invitation had come as a shock, his straitened circumstances alone compelled him to take advantage of any opportunity for free food and drink. He had treated it as a fortuitous oversight on the part of some senile chaperon, but, upon his arrival, was delighted to see that a number of his more dubious acquaintances were in attendance well.

In reply to his cousin's question, however, he was quick to feign surprise and sputter indignantly, "Well, whyever should I not have been included?"

"Gads!" Waverly exclaimed with an expression of mock incredulity. "Never tell me insolvency and lewdness have come into vogue? I had not the least idea! I'm sure I must make a better effort to

16

keep up on the latest crazes. I confess, I feel quite out of touch. However, you must excuse me now—unless deserting one's partner is also in fashion."

If the Marquess of Bastion viewed Lord Waverly's retreating figure with a glare of undisguised malice, another onlooker, although invisible, viewed him with a good deal of more kindly interest. To Lady Sybil's spectral eye, Lord Waverly, whatever his eccentricities might prove to be, seemed to be as much a paragon as Bastion was a scoundrel. Figure, fortune, faculty—and damnably handsome into the bargain: a very likely fellow indeed. Yes, she would keep as close an eye on *him* as well, though for other reasons than his cousin warranted.

Lady Sybil wafted through the crowded ballroom just behind Waverly as he made his way toward her young kinswoman. What a lovely child Lady Selinda was and what a pair she and Lord Waverly made, the ghost thought to herself as the gentleman bowed and led the lady to the floor. A very good match indeed—admittedly more proper than *she* would have liked had her own heart been about to be engaged—but quite the thing for the young lady in question. Nevertheless, Waverly's demeanor promised honor with just a trace of something . . . *interesting*. Lady Sybil smiled complacently as she levitated above the pair.

"A lovely evening, sir," Selinda smiled as she dipped in a low curtsey. She smoothed her pink and white ruffles and gazed up at Waverly with

17

just a hint of sparkle in her intelligent green eyes.

"Made all the lovelier by your presence, I'm sure, Lady Selinda," Waverly returned, surprising himself as he realized that he actually meant his glib compliment. He swallowed hard. What, he wondered, lay behind those sparkling eyes? He took her gloved hand, noting somewhat irrelevantly that it was enticingly delicate and tiny, and stepped into the line of dancers.

"How do you find London?" Waverly asked after a long moment's hesitation. "You have not been long in Town, I collect."

"I am very much afraid," she replied with a sidelong glance from beneath her perilously long lashes, "that I have not found London at all. That is, my dear Aunt Prudence has been plagued with the megrims a good deal since our arrival, and her companion Miss Snypish and I have made our attendance on her our only duty. Indeed, I feared my aunt would not regain her strength in time for the ball tonight and that we must postpone our gathering here. But," Selinda continued with a curving smile that hinted at archness, "the dear thing recovered her health just in time for her last fitting."

"Then you must promise to ride out with me tomorrow and at least see Hyde Park." Waverly again surprised himself. It wasn't often that he saddled himself with young chits during his customarily solitary exercise. Still, as he recalled her aunt's formidable countenance, he would perhaps count the outing as yet another act of charity. Before Selinda could reply, however, the twosome had reached the end of the dance line and were forced to sashay intricately between some five or six other pairs until they found themselves together once again.

"I am sorry, sir, but I do not ride. That is," she corrected, "Aunt does not think it a proper occupation for young ladies. In any case, tomorrow is Sunday and I am certain Aunt Prudence will want my company at morning services."

Waverly made an effort to contain his surprise and barely managed to ask calmly, "Morning *church* services? After a ball?"

"Oh, yes, Aunt would hardly have sanctioned tonight's entertainment had she thought it would interfere in any way with my spiritual well-being. Her son, my cousin Rupert, is in orders, you know, and very generously advises us all in religious matters."

Waverly thought he might have heard the shadow of sarcasm in Selinda's voice, but when he encountered her wide eyes and innocent smile he was *almost* sure he had been mistaken. Perhaps it was just as well that his invitation had been declined, however. He was no rakehell like his cousin, Bastion, but he cherished a firm conviction that virtue as much as vice should be embraced with moderation. Morning church services? After a late night? The idea very nearly made his head spin. But he was curious.

"However will you face the morning, Lady Selinda?" he asked. "Balls, as you know, go on until dawn."

"Do they indeed?" Her brow furrowed delicately

19

in the most fetching way, Waverly thought. "That must be why Aunt Prudence instructed the servants to remove all the spirits at eleven and set out only tea after that. I'm afraid there will be no champagne or punch to be found anywhere in another half-hour."

Waverly suppressed a smile. If Aunt Prudence (an apt name if ever there were one) was hoping to launch her little niece with this sort of entertainment, only the staunchest of suitors would stay on. Once the supplemental flasks in their walking sticks gave out, even these gentlemen would take flight.

"I'm sure the good clergy of London will appreciate your aunt's efforts and pray that she will be a leader among the *ton*," Waverly told her smoothly as the music came to a close. As he bowed over her hand, though, he was not at all certain he wanted to give it up.

"Would you do me the honor of taking a stroll about the room? Surely your next partner can spare you," he told her, deftly taking a peek at the dance card that hung from her wrist. "What good fortune. I see it is just your cousin. Surely a man of the cloth cannot, in charity, begrudge the pleasures of his fellow creatures."

Selinda weighed the consequences of such a disregard of decorum for perhaps the amount of time it took her to bat her pretty eyelashes at his Lordship. "The honor would be mine," she told him with a dimpled smile.

"Some champagne?" he asked as he steered her from the main ballroom.

"I've never tasted champagne before," she told him in a confidential tone. "Aunt always insists on orgeat for me. Is champagne good?"

"My dear child, permit me to make you known to Monsieur le Champagne, a very welcome refugee from the excesses of our French neighbors," he told her in tones that bespoke an exceedingly solemn subject indeed. Deftly, he removed two glasses from the tray of a passing servant. "I promise you, it is very much superior to that cloying syrup with which they so often torture the palates of young ladies. To your health, Lady Selinda."

Selinda took a small sip, opened her eyes very wide, and smiled. "Very much better indeed, Lord Waverly."

"Of course," he went on, "the vintage tonight really is quite excellent. My compliments."

"Oh," Selinda shrugged as she continued to drink her champagne, "that is due more to Aunt Prudence's pinchpenny ways than any sort of developed taste on her part, I assure you. Papa happened to have invested in several cases that were laid down at Darrowdean, our country estate. Though Aunt Prudence does not drink herself, I believe she thought it an excellent notion to provide fine champagne tonight and scrimp on the rest of the refreshments. They are shockingly inadequate as you have no doubt noticed. I know for a fact that it is just whitefish—and very little at that—in the lobster patties."

Waverly looked at her in amazement. Indeed, he did not know when he had come across such forthrightness in a debutante—or any woman for that matter.

"Well, that makes no odds, you know. I doubt any attended tonight for the refreshments."

"Still," she went on in a matter-of-fact tone, "it rankles. I had hoped to make a better showing, but . . ."

"Pray, don't tease yourself, madam. *You* make a very fine showing indeed." As Lady Selinda acknowledged that compliment with a fluttering of her fan, Lord Waverly searched for another topic of conversation. He knew he really ought to return her to her party, but was strangely loath to do so. "You lost your parents quite recently, I believe."

"Yes, it has only been two years," she told him, the lovely sparkle prompted by the champagne slowly fading from her eyes. "We have just come out of mourning quite recently."

"My condolences," he murmured, cursing himself for allowing the conversation to take such a turn. Selinda stared reflectively into space for a time.

"I imagine it's time you returned me to my aunt," she smiled after a moment.

"I'm so terribly sorry to have brought up such a melancholy memory," he told her remorsefully. "I assure you I am not often such a flat."

"Oh, it isn't that, Lord Waverly," she reassured him. "Indeed, I appreciate your concern. It seems that so very few ever acknowledge another's loss. They prattle on and pretend that nothing has happened. It's only," she went on, "that I happened just now to remark my cousin's expression. He seems not to be of so charitable a bent as you imagined. I do believe that if I had been a glass of new milk, I should have been much in danger of curdling just now."

As Waverly escorted her back to her party, he shuddered inwardly. Here was assembled a rogue's gallery! Indeed, the group resembled as grim-faced a set as Hogarth ever invented in his caricatures of villainy personified: the aunt, framed by an appalling conglomeration of lavender and puce silk, was as bloated and pale as a cellar spider. The companion hovering at her side was a sallow, emaciated stick wrapped in gray lace. Cousin Rupert loomed hugely in the background, bulging repulsively in his too tight pantaloons. All of them were frowning.

How in Heaven's name, Waverly wondered, had this sweet young thing found her way into the cold bosom of this altogether unsightly and ungracious set? Any suitor would have to be more than a little hearty to brave their disparaging glances. Indeed, the threesome barely condescended to nod their heads in acknowledgment of him as he handed his partner into her chair.

"Lady Selinda," the whey-faced Miss Snypish began with a nasal whine, "your aunt desires that you remain here with us during the next few sets. You will overtire yourself and you are so very delicate."

Selinda looked rebelliously at her aunt. She was not, nor had she ever been, in the least delicate. "But my card is full!" she protested in an un-

23

dertone. "It would be the grossest bad manners to disappoint these gentlemen particularly at my own ball!"

"Never thought nothing of disappointing *me*," her cousin muttered with venomous bad grace.

Gads, what an unattractive young man, Waverly shuddered with a mental grimace. It was all he could do to keep from raising his quizzing glass to examine this specimen further. Then, he noticed the deep blush of embarrassment rising in Selinda's cheeks. The kindest thing he could do at this point, he decided, would be to bow his respects and retreat as quietly as possible.


Lady Sybil had observed the scene with no small amount of indignation. Just who were these awful people and how did they come to exert such control over Selinda? From their looks they were certainly not Harrowebys, unless the stock had taken a violent downswing. Harrowebys might not always have been the most virtuous of families, but they had invariably been an attractive one.

As the ghost reflected, it seemed that her task might not be so much to keep the child out of the clutches of such rakes as Bastion (for it seemed unlikely that even he would be equal to such squinty scrutiny as this tribe exhibited), but to put her in the path of such worthies as Lord Waverly without interference. It appeared that this self-commission would be a challenge indeed.

Lady Sybil settled herself above a potted palm where she could observe goings-on about the room. Lady Selinda's eyes flashed and she fanned herself with a vigor born of sheer vexation. The Marquess of Bastion sidled toward her party with an ambitious ogle. From a distance, Lord Waverly observed the whole with a look of puzzled but keen interest. At least, Lady Sybil decided, the stage was set for a fine theatrical: but would it be tragedy, comedy, or farce?

# Chapter Three

The last guest departed Harroweby House at the unfashionable hour of just five minutes past midnight, and an extremely disgruntled crowd it had been for more reasons than just the sudden scandalous dearth of champagne and punch. Because balls customarily ran well into the small hours of the morning, the guests had quite naturally made no other plans and had accepted no other invitations. Thus they were most displeased to find themselves out on the street in the shank of the evening with no place to go. Moreover, not only had several mamas seen their budding daughters wrenched from what they judged to be very promising flirtations, but their overextended papas were now ruing the expense of new gowns, fans, and slippers worn to so little purpose.

All in all, the guests vowed both privately and publicly that there never was such a miscarriage of manners as at Harroweby House that night. It was, of course, quite a pity about Lady Selinda, who seemed a sprightly thing, but her noxious family was not to be borne.

Selinda watched the ball disintegrate about her with a set polite smile on her face which concealed a heart bursting with humiliation and longing for revenge. Although she had neither sanctioned nor promoted her aunt's directive for curtailing the "strong waters" that evening, Selinda had naively thought that some guests would linger on. Indeed, a few of the more forebearing variety had, but prompted by Aunt Prudence's cavernous yawns and constant, ill-bred consultation of her son's timepiece, the gathering had become smaller and smaller with each advancement of the minute hand. Then, after the most steadfast of Selinda's suitors had secured her aunt's grudging permission to call, even they had faded into the night along with the rest.

While Selinda remained unwavering in her apparent tranquility, the invisible Lady Sybil indulged her own raging frustration, pacing about several feet off the floor and making the almost-deserted ballroom quite icy with her displeasure.

"Egads, Mater," the offensive Rupert shuddered, his corpulent person quivering unpleasantly, "I'm almost frozen in this drafty vault of a ballroom."

"Poor suffering Rupert!" his mother exclaimed, chafing his ample face vigorously between her two hands until it was quite mottled. "What you don't put up with on your selfish cousin's behalf. She *must* have a ball, so have a ball she does. And that is not enough, but she must insult my poor Rupert as well. Well, I hope you have enjoyed this little party, Selinda, for I vow it shall be the last. I am sure I must take to my bed for the next fortnight, at the very least. And poor Rupert, too. I declare, you've gone quite flushed, Rupert, my love."

"But I *feel* quite pale, Mater," he frowned pettishly, improving his looks not one whit. "I feel p'raps I have an ague coming on. Indeed, I don't believe I shall make services in the morning."

"No more do I, pet," his mother concurred mournfully, "and it grieves me sorely. Here, have a macaroon, my love. You need some sustenance. Miss Snypish, you shall accompany Lady Selinda to church in the morning. I think the early service will do best, for I shall be wanting you most of the day."

Miss Snypish nodded briefly, her eyes narrow with satisfaction and her mouth set in an unbecoming thin line. "I shall see that her Ladyship rises at a goodly hour, madam."

"And see, Selinda, that you give good thought to your spiritual faults, such as selfishness and pride," Rupert added, chewing his macaroon vigorously. As he did so, Selinda endeavored valiantly to evade the crumbs that erupted from his mouth. It was all she could do to withstand the understandable temptation to pull her skirts above her head for protection.

"I shall select some pertinent verses for you to meditate on tomorrow," he continued when he had swallowed. "It grieves me—more than you will ever know—to be critical of you, dearest cousin, but I daresay I give a good deal more thought to your spiritual well-being than you do yourself."

Selinda sighed and bowed her head, but Lady Sybil noted with some satisfaction that the young lady's fists were tightly clenched.

"Now give heed to Rupert, Selinda," Aunt Prudence admonished sternly, wagging her finger at the girl in a singularly annoying manner. "Your frivolous nature may chafe, but you may be sure he has your soul's good at heart."

Selinda looked up serenely enough, though after a long pause, and replied with a disarming smile, "Indeed, good aunt and cousin, I am sure you both give *my* soul far more attention than your own. Pray give me leave to retire to my chamber then that I might reflect on this sinful nature with which I am burdened."

"Well," her aunt sniffed, "I hope you will not forget us in your prayers. Now give your cousin a kiss goodnight for all his kindness."

At this, Rupert stepped forward with a good deal more alacrity than would have been thought possible for one of his girth; he would, indeed, have planted a kiss directly on Selinda's lips had she not quickly turned her head and presented him with her cheek instead. In spite of this diversionary tactic, his sticky mouth remained moistly in place a great deal longer than was necessary while his plump hands pressed with presumptuous urgency at her slim waist. Selinda pulled herself away as quickly as she could, resisting the overwhelming urge to wipe her cheek with her handkerchief then and there. Steeling herself, however, she bid them all a terse good night, her expression as unreadable as ever, but her cheeks blazing.

Lady Sybil followed Selinda from the room and watched as the girl's countenance became increasingly wrathful with each stair she mounted. Once she had gained her own chamber and carefully shut the door behind her, Selinda wrenched off her gown, trampling it in a heap on the floor. Then in a great flurry, she pulled the pins and bows from her hair, angrily shook out her curls, and threw herself forcefully onto the bed. There, at last, she furiously pounded her fists into the pillows until the feathers flew about her in an angry blizzard. When her first frenzy had passed, she lay still for a moment trying to catch her breath. "Count," she whispered to herself in measured tones, "one, two, three, four, five . . ."

She closed her eyes resolutely and concentrated on taking deep breaths. Selinda had very nearly regained her composure when the supercilious visage of her cousin Rupert rose up in her mind. "If only I could stick an apple in that sticky mouth to complete the piggish picture!" she whispered in vicious tones. Suppressing a frustrated oath, the girl rolled instead onto her back and kicked her kid slippers across the length of the room. Then she beat an angry rhythm into the mattress with her feet as she pulled a pillow over her face and released a muffled groan.

Lady Sybil, who had floated silently up to the

canopy, was more than a little afraid that her descendent might be carried off in a fit of apoplexy that very night, and little wonder. However, it was a relief that Selinda had finally evidenced (to an alarming degree, admittedly) some of the frustration her ghostly observer had been feeling on her behalf all evening.

When Selinda had finally lain calmly for several silent minutes, the door from the adjoining closet opened softly and a pale, wide-eyed face appeared gingerly around the corner.

"Is the fit over yet?" a small whisper came.

"Yes, Lucy," Selinda sighed wearily, sitting up on the edge of the bed. "You may enter without fear of flying gowns, shoes, or tempers."

At that, a small figure in a long white nightrail crept into the room and climbed up on the bed beside Selinda. "Was it terrible bad tonight?"

"Bad enough, little sister," Selinda grimaced in distaste. Then she sighed. "Some parts were quite lovely, though."

"Did you dance with a mysterious, handsome man?"

"I danced with several men, pet, handsome and homely, but none of them terribly mysterious, I'm afraid. The dancing part was lovely. But then! *Then*, Aunt Prudence and Rupert all but pushed the guests out the door with their wretched manners. Oh, Lucy," she whispered in hushed tones, "it was awful! I fear I shall never be received anywhere after this, I shall never have an offer, and I shall be forced to marry Rupert!"

"Do not say that, Selinda!" Lucy reproached her

sister sternly. "You are not meant for the likes of that oafish pig!"

"Lucy!" she hissed urgently. "Have a care! If one of those snakes should hear you, they would send you away to boarding school for certain and I know I could not bear it here without my brave little sister!"

"Have faith," Lucy whispered confidently, as she snuggled in as best she could beneath the thin, threadbare coverlet. "We shall not ever be parted except by some good fortune. Mama and Papa may be up in heaven and fiends from hell in their stead, but we shall be looked after, Selinda. I know it indeed."

"Strange child," Selinda murmured as she tucked her sister into bed and drew an extra shawl up over her chin. "You always sound so sure of yourself. Have you had another of your dreams?"

"Yes, and it was a grand one!" Lucy exclaimed, sitting up in bed again. "Aunt Prudence frothed with a ferocious fit, Rupert ended head down in a mucky ditch, and you—this is the very best part of it!—you married a mysterious, handsome, kind gentleman! All because of a lovely lady who looks after us. I wonder who she is?"

"I do not know, Lucy, but I pray you are right. In any case, it sounds like a marvelous dream." Selinda smoothed her sister's black braids on the pillow and kissed her on the forehead. Lucy, she knew, was a very special child. Not only was she exceedingly bright for her age, but, from the time she was a toddler, Lucy had had a curious way of predicting the future and guessing one's thoughts.

Selinda had come to accept it; however, knowing that others might find the talent unnerving, she had made the child promise to keep it to herself. "Now, shall I read to you for a bit from our book?"

"Oh, yes, Selinda! I have been waiting all day. We had just got to an exciting part when that devil Snypish burst in on us last night!"

"Well, I've taken precautions tonight, my love. Look—I've fit our little novel into my prayer-book cover. Our self-righteous custodians can surely have no objections if we read a few psalms before bedtime."

"Why, Selinda," Lucy giggled as she nestled against her sister, "aren't you a sly one!"

"I have need to be, goose! Now where were we? Ah, yes! Here we are. Chapter Eighteen. *'In the moonlight, fair Rosamonde leaned from her bower, breathing in the rich perfume of the warm summer's eve. Her ringlets fell about her ivory shoulders in a golden cascade, tumbling over the edge of the balcony and delicately plaiting themselves into the winding red roses that grew beneath. Alas! All this beauty was insufficient to distract the poor maiden from her perilous plight. Rosamonde shut her teary eyes for a moment against the bright moonbeams, praying for strength.*

"*'Ah me!' she sighed heavily, raising one eloquent hand to her brow. 'Is there no help for me? Is there no hope? Is there no champion who can free me from this monstrous tangle of evil intent?'*

"*'You have but to ask, fair maid!' came a voice*

*alarmingly close to her ear.*

"'Rosamonde in an instant opened her eyes and beheld a masked stranger who had boldly invaded the privacy of her meditations. Pierced to the heart at such forwardness (yet intrigued at the same time by his apparent nobility and charm), she could neither flee nor cry out, but immediately sank in a swoon, one arm still bent back against her alabaster brow and the other draped modestly across her creamy bosom.

"'The bandit, for so he seemed, bent forward and kissed her gently on the lips, saying, "My love, oft have I seen from afar the wickedness, the perfidy that even now threatens you and I shall take you far from here where none can ever presume such evil upon your fair person again." And lifting her up as if she were but merest thistledown, he stepped onto the ledge and dropped lightly on the waiting steed beneath . . .'"*

"Selinda?" Lucy interrupted, her brows knit. "Why must the ladies always swoon at the best part? I vow I shouldn't!"

"Why you forward thing," Selinda laughed. "Well, I don't imagine I should either, truth to tell. But it's a lovely story, don't you think?"

"I don't believe it is a story," Lucy protested, "all except the swooning part. You shall see when you have your adventure!"

"Well, there is little likelihood of that, unfortunately. But I vow I shall escape this trap if I possibly can, and take you with me. I am grateful our affairs were left orderly enough when Mama and Papa died that we were at least each assured a

34

Season when we turned eighteen. At least we have a chance. And, even if it is just the Little Season, Aunt Prudence will not be able to ruin it altogether, however much she's tampered with other things. What's more, I promise you, Lucy," her voice dropping to a whisper as she crossed her heart, "I shall take the first offer that's made me."

"Oh, don't think of doing that, Selinda!" Lucy protested, sitting up. "Please don't!"

"I begin to fear I must, Lucy. There really is no other choice. Anyone is better than Rupert! Now, you must close your eyes and go to sleep, and I must set this room to rights."

Lady Sybil watched indignantly as Selinda picked up her own gown and slippers and put them tidily away. Clearly the poor child was not even allowed a lady's maid! As she looked more closely about the room, it was evident that the girls were forced to make do with the barest and poorest of furnishings. Well, this would never do. Something would simply have to be done, that much was certain, and not a moment to lose!

# Chapter Four

As a matter of pride, Selinda arose the next morning at the first sound of the awakening birds that thrived in the trees outside her window. She did not, however, immediately address herself to her toilette, but instead sat for several moments in the window seat, watching the environs busily awake to a new day. How different from Darrowdean and its seclusion! Selinda and Lucy had rarely been away from the country estate in all their growing-up years, and living in the city with all its noises was one more adjustment.

During those years, their parents had but rarely been at home. Their mother, an invalid of some renown, divided her time between spas and watering spots, while their father took what pleasure might be found in hunting and riding in the surrounding area. They returned to Darrowdean once or twice a year, expressed surprise that their children were growing up so rapidly, and departed almost as quickly. Granted, during their stay, they lavished gifts on the girls and dressed them like a pair of dolls, but these visits were always somehow unreal.

The girls had, of course, been committed to the care of an army of servants and tutors, but among that group there had been none for whom they felt any particular ties. The staff had been efficient but distant. For those reasons, Selinda and Lucy had depended upon each other for companionship and solace. They had fussed over each other, planned and dreamed together. They each felt a little guilty for not feeling their parents' loss more keenly, but, truthfully, until the arrival of their unsavory guardians, little in their lives had changed.

Selinda pulled herself abruptly from these absent musings and performed her simple toilette listening to the complexity of the starlings' chirping chorus. As she did so, she wondered, not for the first time, how such ugly, speckled birds could contrive to produce such sweet music. As she spied one trilling away on a narrow branch, she shook her head. Its beady little eyes, scrawny form, and unremarkable plumage reminded her all too forcibly of the rattleboned Miss Snypish. Well, she thought, hurrying herself, she was not about to give that offensive person the satisfaction (and pleasure, she deduced) of finding her unready.

In spite of the fortune to which she was heiress, Lady Selinda's wardrobe was not an extensive one. In the name of repressing vanity, Aunt Prudence had given away (or sold, as Lucy suspected) most of Selinda's wardrobe when she arrived to assume her nieces' guardianship. Little deliberation was necessary, therefore, in order for Selinda to select a simple dress of deep indigo.

The dress was something of a secret triumph for Selinda, chiefly because she knew Aunt Prudence had chosen the style and somber color in order to set her at odds with fashion and custom. Although it had been cut along what Aunt Prudence deemed to be modest lines, high-necked and long-sleeved, it could not have been more flattering. The row of stiff ruffles at the neck made her face seem almost heart-shaped, and the color, far too deep a shade for a girl embarking on her first season, reflected in her green eyes and produced a startling aquamarine hue. The absence of any suspicion of puffs or superfluous draping failed in its attempt at severity and served merely to accentuate her trim figure.

The first time Aunt Prudence had seen Selinda in the dress, her face had puckered in an unmerciful frown. It was all Selinda could do to suppress the laughter that momentarily threatened to bubble to the surface as she sensed her aunt's inner debate: Should the dress be discarded as too flattering or kept to avert further expenditure? Frugality had won the day.

Selinda had just secured her last button when Miss Snypish burst unceremoniously into the chamber. She stopped in her tracks at the sight of Selinda, clearly betimes in her preparation.

"Oh," the companion managed to mutter disconsolately. The disappointment at having missed the chance to rouse a comfortable sleeper was clearly reflected in the deepening lines which decorated that lady's already distressing countenance. Selinda would have been much surprised had she known that Miss Letitia Snypish was not

38

a contemporary of Aunt Prudence; however, her grim expression, austere deportment, and conservative attitudes made her seem far older than her mere seven and twenty years of age. "I see you've managed to stir yourself after all," was the woman's ungracious comment.

Selinda lowered her eyelashes primly. "Indeed, I made a special point of it. I would not think of discommoding *you* for all the world, Miss Snypish."

"I daresay," she was answered in a sarcastic tone. Miss Snypish looked Selinda up and down as though searching for a fault. "Bareheaded?!" she demanded suddenly, her eyes gleaming with mean satisfaction.

Selinda quickly produced a bonnet of black straw trimmed with violet ruching and tied its wide satin bow at an angle which just missed being jaunty. "Far be it from me to disregard the dictates of St. Paul," she smiled with devout ingenuousness.

"Prayer book?" Miss Snypish snapped with unmistakable annoyance. Selinda crossed quickly to the bedside and grabbed her prayer book from the nightstand, silently uttering a very fervent prayer indeed that the companion would not be infernally inspired to examine its unauthorized contents. As she turned back, however, she noticed the shrew bearing down on Lucy's sleeping figure.

"Miss Snypish!" she whispered urgently, "Pray do not wake Lucy!" Selinda was willing enough to sacrifice her own repose for the peace of the household, but she was concerned about her little sister, whom she feared was quite delicate. It had been a late night for the child, and Selinda had sensed her fitful dreaming. She had to think quickly. "I would have aroused her myself, of course, but since my aunt did not specifically include the child in her instructions, I did not wish to take such an action upon myself. Perhaps Aunt will have need of Lucy's companionship while we are gone this morning."

"Need?" Miss Snypish snorted disdainfully. "Of that baggage?"

With a concerted effort of will, Selinda bit her tongue and fixed an expression of innocence on her face. "Of course you must know best, Miss Snypish, as always. Perhaps you would like to step down the hall, wake Aunt Prudence, and ask her . . . just to make sure."

Glaring contemptuously at Selinda, Miss Snypish turned abruptly from the sleeping figure and made for the door. "Well, don't dilly-dally," she spat and exited without further ceremony. Selinda followed, her emotions teetering between relief and dread.

The dampening chill of the early hour in which Selinda and Miss Snypish shivered as they walked to morning services also greeted the bleary-eyed figure of Lord Waverly as he emerged from Boodle's. He had spent the remainder of the night dividing his time between the gaming tables and an excellent bottle of brandy as his brain teased itself over the odd events of the evening. His Lordship had not yet been to bed nor was he, in spite of his fatigue, ready to repair there.

Lord Waverly was troubled, and even Boodle's various amusements had done little to distract him from the memory of two particularly lovely green eyes which had been on the brink of spilling over with tears when last he saw them. He sat himself down on the club's front stoop, oblivious to the picture he presented, set his chin in his hand, and pondered the conundrum. Damme, he thought to himself, there was something exceedingly unsavory about the little family portrait he had studied last night at Harroweby House. Something clearly did not fit and that something was Lady Selinda. The guests had been an oddly sorted crew at best, and the hosts themselves all but bristled with wretched breeding and incivility. Only Lady Selinda stood out as a paragon of beauty, gentility, grace, and humor. In Lord Waverly's experience, such Incomparables did not spring inexplicably from such unrefined surroundings. No, his heart told him, something was amiss indeed.

Just at this moment, he felt a soft pressure against his leg and looked down to see that a small orange kitten with an oddly wrinkled ear had joined him. He picked it up and began to pet it absently, its gratified purring providing apt music for his meditations. He turned over the information and impressions he had been able to glean thus far. None of it fit. The girl, after all, was the heiress, the one with the potential to eventually benefit those who now held the reins of power. Typically, persons whose access to wealth rested in the good graces of their wards gradually became less dictatorial and more fawning as their charges approached adulthood. That clearly was not the case here. There was no evidence in particular to which Waverly could point, but it was his decided opinion that the lovely Lady Selinda, in spite of her momentary outburst, was not only merely submissive to her guardians but terrified of them as well.

There was something else, too. Thus far, he could only describe it as "the mask," but Waverly was convinced that there was a good deal more to Lady Selinda than met the eye. The surface she presented was, of course, unobjectionable. Indeed, if ever a face cried out to be memorialized in ivory, it was hers. But beneath that lovely, seemingly serene demeanor, something *else* had momentarily shone through. Something had briefly sparkled and flashed until better judgment, born of who knew what jeopardy, forced it to withdraw behind a mask of false composure. Disconcerted but intrigued, Waverly breathed in the morning air and sighed. He raised the kitten up and stared into its blue eyes. "Can't make heads nor tails of it, cat."

The kitten vouchsafed a small, plaintive wail which sounded for all the world like commiseration, and planted its small, sharp claws in the superfine cloth of his Lordship's lapels. "No more can you, eh? Well, my dear fellow, we shall just have to put our heads to it."

His footman, having been speedily aroused and sent round to do his master's bidding, slowed his progress momentarily as he perceived his employer apparently engaged in an earnest discussion with a mangy kitten. Frowning inwardly at this lack of comportment, he presented himself nonetheless with an impeccable bow. "The horses are being

42

harnessed now, your Lordship. It will be just a moment."

"No matter, Richard," Waverly shrugged, waving off his attendance and handing him the kitten. "Take care of this little beast."

Holding the squirming animal away from his immaculate livery and pinching it at the scruff of its neck between his thumb and forefinger, Richard grimaced eloquently. "I am afraid I do not perfectly understand, my lord."

"Why, take the brute home, feed it, and set it in front of a mousehole," Waverly told him with an admirably straight face. "I, on the other hand, shall walk this morning. When you've settled my Lord Whiskers here, go back to bed. Sorry to have inconvenienced you."

As the said Richard watched his master saunter off into the dim morning, he glared menacingly at the kitten. It was outside of enough to be charged with the care of this wretched creature, but it was more than that. The very idea of being apologized to by his betters brought his indignation to an even higher pitch. Of all the degrading insults, he fumed to himself. It went against the natural order of things, after all. If *he* could remember *his* place, certainly his Lordship ought to try to do the same. Only the outlandishly high wages he was paid kept him from being completely overborne by the outrages which accompanied employment by the likes of an eccentric like Lord Waverly. Pulling up his collar against the damp and depositing the kitten in his pocket, Richard heaved a sigh of relief as he reflected that at least there had been no witnesses this time.

*　　　*　　　*

As Waverly continued to walk, his musings on the affairs of the previous night kept pace with him. He had no clear destination in mind, only the vague notion that some brisk exercise would clear his head sufficiently to tackle this conundrum. All around him the sounds of London awakening filled the air: the clip-clop of horses' hooves on cobblestone, the rasp of brooms clearing away a night's worth of dirt from doorsteps, the resolute peals of church bells calling out to the faithful. In spite of his weariness, the clear sounds and the astringent air of morning made Waverly grateful he was not among the snoring numbers of the *ton;* however, he reflected with a large yawn, once a month at most would be sufficient to rejuvenate his spirit.

As he proceeded on his stroll, Waverly drew a few veiled stares from the early rising household staffs as they went about their business. They were not, of course, unaccustomed to witnessing the disheveled remnants of an evening's debauchery making their unsteady way home, but generally these gentlemen were assisted by their long-suffering drivers and grooms, then smuggled in back doors, their hats pulled low, and their faces already reflecting the misery with which their much-abused heads and stomachs would soon repay them.

Instead, Lord Waverly's evening clothes, however inappropriate for the hour, were still pristine; he smiled blandly and tipped his hat to passing maids, and his gait grew jauntier with each step he took. Absolutely disgraceful, they thought to themselves as he passed by. The gentry were due their pleasures, of course, but anyone with an ounce of decency had a duty to suffer in recompense. No shame at all!

Oblivious to this silent disapproval, Lord Waverly had unconsciously followed the summons of the church bells and soon found himself among a small procession intent on Grosvenor Chapel. He slowed his pace and drew aside to a stone bench where he sat for a time watching the people pass by. It was still far too early for any of the fashionable set to be about; these seemed for the most part to be the families of tradesmen, displaying varying degrees of prosperity. He frowned as he realized how little attention the gentry (himself included) paid to this portion of society on whom they depended for so much of their comfort and security. But as far as most of his circle was concerned, the rest of the world was invisible.

As he scanned the scene, his attention was riveted by a familiar pair about to make their way inside the church: Lady Selinda Harroweby and that depressing . . . Miss Snipchin, was it? Slyfish? Something quite appropriate, he recalled. Perhaps he would remember later. Suddenly inspired, he pulled himself up, mounted the steps, and stole quietly into the back of the church.

# *Chapter Five*

Although wide awake, Lucy had lain quite still in bed all the while Selinda and the regrettable Miss Snypish engaged in that morning's brief verbal sparring. She certainly would not have begrudged Selinda, whom she quite adored, whatever small comfort her company might have provided; sad experience, however, had taught Lucy well. She knew that her wicked inability to govern her yawns and fidgets during church services had resulted more often than not in odious punishments not only for Lucy, but her sister as well. Under the circumstances, Lucy decided that feigned slumber was by far her wisest course.

Lazing about in bed, however, was by no means a part of Lucy's plan for the day. A dreadful cacophony of snores (which might well have terrified a less intrepid soul!) issued loudly from the wing occupied by Aunt Prudence and Cousin Rupert: to Lucy's finely tuned ears, however, their racket sounded as sweet as any symphony, for, with Miss Snypish absent as well, it signaled a rare respite from her guardians' repressive surveillance. While the noxious pair slept, therefore, the child quickly prepared herself to explore the corridors and nooks of her relatively new surroundings.

A fortnight earlier, Lucy had been engaged in just such a tour when her investigations had been rudely interrupted. Finding herself unwatched for a moment in the bustle of moving into Harroweby House, Lucy had availed herself of this singular occasion to look about her ancestral home. The original section of the house had been constructed several centuries earlier, at that time well outside of the city proper. Over the years, however, London's population had burgeoned and only a few acres of the original park now surrounded the house. The structure itself had changed with the times as well, as the personality and taste of each ensuing heir resulted in the building of additional wings and new facades until the house had become at length a sprawling conglomeration of architectural history and personal idiosyncrasy.

Lucy had tackled the maze systematically, beginning by visiting each of the rooms in the east wing and poking into each of the countless alcoves and crannies. The halls echoed noisily even in response to her small footsteps, for they were largely empty, Aunt Prudence having not only sent much of the furnishings to storage (or so she *said*) but also having determined to run the house with less than half of the necessary staff. Lucy had been engaged in her circuitous explorations for some time when she finally came upon the main gallery where she stopped to examine a long series of what appeared to be family portraits. As she gazed into their shadowy depths, she felt her spine suddenly begin to prickle and her heart grow cold. This peculiar psychic phenomenon was followed forthwith by the more tangible iron grip of Miss Snypish digging cruelly into her little shoulder.

"What do you mean by sneaking off in that sly way, you wicked little creature?" the pinch-faced companion had snarled, giving her a shake. "I have been looking about for you this hour!"

"Beg pardon, Miss Snypish," Lucy had automatically returned, bowing her head in a gallingly submissive manner as Selinda had so often drilled her.

Miss Snypish surveyed her with a speculative frown. "I wonder indeed what impish tricks you are up to, you vile little insect! Do not imagine you can hide anything from me. I can see by the glint in your eyes you are on the verge of some unholy mischief!"

"Indeed, Miss Snypish, I meant no harm. I knew I ought not to be underfoot today, and I have never had the occasion to see these portraits before. Besides," Lucy could not help adding in an innocent voice, "I know I am not as schooled as *you* in the ways of sin, but I could see no wickedness in looking about *my* home."

At that, Miss Snypish's visage turned a decidedly unhealthy shade of mauve. "Schooled in the ways of sin!" she sputtered angrily. "We shall see, Little Lady. We shall see. I collect now that you are of a very delicate turn of health, and I hear reports that some religious boarding schools devote themselves to the soul at the expense of the body's worldly cares. Their rigors are not said to be at all conducive to longevity. Yes, Lady Lucy, we shall see indeed."

Forced thus to abandon her exciting expedition, Lucy had ignored the thinly veiled threat with characteristic fortitude; however, withdrawing from the gallery, she had wistfully taken one last glance at a particular portrait that had riveted her attention. How she had longed to show it to Selinda!

Thus it was when she finally heard the front door close behind Miss Snypish and her sister, Lucy sprang forthwith from the bed and swiftly replaited her straight black hair before donning her simple lavender frock and gray pinafore. Glancing in the mirror, she grimaced automatically at her odd little reflection. Selinda might kindly describe her features as elfin, but Lucy knew quite well that her hazel eyes were far too large for her angular little face, her complexion too colorless, and her smile too crooked. No, she was all too aware that she would never be the great beauty her sister was, but at least she had her precious gift of second sight which was growing increasingly clear with each passing day—more clear than she had as yet admitted to Selinda.

Silently quitting the chamber she shared with her sister, Lucy tiptoed down the long corridor, then flew down the staircase and made a swift pass through the dining room where she selected a few pieces of fruit and some biscuits. Then she quietly found her way to the back staircase and up again to the gallery where her last expedition had been so suddenly curtailed. She was a methodical child, for all her ten years, and in no time at all, she had located the exact painting she had been admiring when the interfering Miss Snypish had so irksomely pounced on her.

Lucy inhaled deeply as she drank in the sight before her. It was a remarkable portrait indeed, for the woman depicted therein was the very image of her sister Selinda. The resemblance was not at first pronounced, however, for the subject was costumed in a decidedly antiquated manner. The uncanny duplicate of her sister's familiar face was haloed by a froth of careless ringlets hung with pearls; a patch in the shape of a crescent moon accented the upturned corners of the lady's mouth. A filigreed pomander in the shape of a pear studded with pearls rested snugly between her breasts, and yards of rose velvet caught up with elaborate clusters of pearls cascaded elegantly into a graceful train. One hand grasped a small white rose; the other was delicately uplifted, forming a perch for an exquisitely feathered cockatiel.

Although Lucy had admired the portrait excessively from the first and had been impatient to look upon it again, she was now captured by it for quite another reason than its resemblance to Selinda: the subject of the portrait, now that she was able to inspect it for several minutes, was the very woman who had figured so importantly in her dream of several nights earlier. She sat herself down on the floor and stared contentedly into the painting's depths, munching slowly on a biscuit she had pulled from her pocket. This is the lady who looks after us, Lucy affirmed happily to herself.

Lady Sybil had floated along after Lucy since the child's arising, and stood some time now lost in poignant thought as she regarded her portrait taken more than a century ago. The artist, an Italian of devastatingly good looks (which had very nearly equaled his artistic prowess) had been quite abandoned in his admiration for her. Now she contemplated with a good deal of pleasant recollection (and not, to be sure, the least whisper of shame) the source of the glowing rosiness which embellished her complexion in his masterpiece. Indeed, the artist had taken extraordinary pains to examine at breathtakingly close proximity the intricate pearl pomander which nestled so cozily in her bosom before he rendered it in painstaking detail. This artistic conscientiousness had added a good three months to Umberto's already lengthy stay at Harroweby House. She smiled nostalgically at the memory of their time together and heaved a deep sigh.

As she did so, Lucy turned around and stared, her eyes and mouth opened wide. Lady Sybil automatically looked over her shoulder. No one was there. Turning back to Lucy once more, she saw that the child's expression of shock had turned to one of sheer felicity.

"It's you!" Lucy whispered, awestruck.

❋     ❋     ❋

The air inside the church was heavy with the scent of beeswax and incense: the odor of sanctity, Lord Waverly thought whimsically. Making his way quietly up the aisle and slipping surreptitiously into the pew immediately behind her, he settled himself comfortably and set about contemplating the exquisite Lady Selinda Harroweby at his leisure. He was quite confident it would be a religious experience.

It had been Waverly's studied opinion for at least eight hours now that Lady Selinda's sylph-like beauty was without question altogether unparalleled; however, the inescapable comparison occasioned by the proximity of Miss Snypish's frightful profile forcibly brought to mind every myth his Lordship had ever heard of goddesses made mortal. Did Lady Selinda's dainty feet touch the ground when she walked? Would not her kiss transform mere mortal men to enchanted thralls? And would not such bondage be worth the ecstasy that delicious moment, however fleeting, might bring?

Waverly shook himself reproachfully. Clearly, the combination of a sleepless night, more brandy than was absolutely wise, and, yes, the delicate effect which sunlight filtered through stained glass had on a perfect, dewy complexion were leading him to flights of fancy. Such whimsical notions were not unknown to him, of course, but he had learned long since to be wary of them, particularly where the fair sex was concerned.

Waverly wrenched himself from these highly entertaining musings, therefore, and instead forced himself to concentrate on one detail which he had heretofore studiously disregarded: Lady Selinda's conspicuous religious fervor. As the service progressed, she gazed fixedly into the depths of her prayer book with admirable (and daunting) diligence. Two bright spots of pink burned eloquently in her cheeks. Yes, the girl was lovely beyond all measure, Waverly sighed inwardly, but he was sinkingly sure that the unusual degree of solemn spirituality she displayed here would be altogether incompatible with the frivolous romantic images he had just abandoned.

Selinda's concentration on her prayer book, however much it dampened Lord Waverly's interest, now drew the curiosity of the entire congregation, for she was entirely oblivious when the last strains of the hymn issuing from the choir loft faded away into silence. Although the rest of the congregation had obediently taken their seats, Selinda remained rapt and upright, turning the pages of her prayer book with slow deliberation. A low chorus of whispers began to rise.

*. . . and as fair Rosamonde rested her golden tresses on Lord Ravenstock's broad shoulders,* Selinda was reading, *she inadvertently raised her ruby lips to his. Lord Ravenstock murmured an oath and crushed her to him in an embrace both powerful and —*

"Lady Selinda!" Miss Snypish interrupted suddenly in a hateful hiss. "You are making a spectacle of yourself! Sit down at once!"

Still, Selinda remained apparently engrossed by her religious meditations. Realizing with growing irritation that her communication had fallen on deaf ears, Miss Snypish grimaced, leaned forward, and, unwisely, delivered a deliberately cruel pinch to Selinda's arm. If Miss Snypish had expected that her action would in any way divert the crowd's growing interest in Selinda's odd behavior, she could not have been more mistaken.

Although Miss Snypish had fully intended her pinch to be as painful as she could contrive, she had not counted on the dramatic nature of its immediate consequences. The moment her scrawny fingers had closed with such brutal precision on the soft flesh of her charge's forearm, Selinda had instinctively cried out in a most resonant and singular manner, forcibly reminding several members of the fascinated congregation of their terrifying encounters with savages in the colonies.

And if this piercing cry were not sufficient, the attack had so surprised Selinda that she simultaneously let fly her little prayer book. Its swift trajectory made an abrupt arc as it sailed up over her head and came almost immediately fluttering down into the pew directly behind, landing with a resounding thud at the feet of an exceedingly astonished Lord Waverly.

The chapel was now absolutely silent, the congregation's eyes trained as one on this remarkable exhibition. Selinda, suddenly aware of the spectacle she had created, slowly looked about at her entranced audience and turned a impressive shade of magenta. If only she had remembered to remove her little novel from the prayer book's cover, she berated herself inwardly, this catastrophe would never have taken place! Just then, Miss Snypish bent down as if to retrieve the wayward article, and Selinda's heightened color faded just as quickly as it had arisen, her cheeks whitening with horror at the prospect of discovery. Without stopping a moment to think, she made a precipitate (and thoroughly unladylike) lunge under the pew just as Lord Waverly did the same. Thus it was that the pair found themselves suddenly face to face, underneath the pew, their lips separated by a mere inch.

Afterward Lord Waverly could never quite explain what had come over him, except that the sudden sight and proximity of so lovely a face quite overset him. He had, after all, just spent the greater part of a long night engaged in conjuring up its lovely features. Regardless of logical explanations (or lack thereof) Lord Waverly simply leaned forward just the least bit further and kissed Selinda full on the lips.

Selinda's recent meditations had, of course, been no less worldly than his Lordship's; moreover, his handsome features had impressed themselves on her more deeply than she had allowed herself to admit the night before. Even though the sardonic hero of her novel was described therein as having hair and eyes as black as midnight, it was Lord Waverly's dark blue eyes and carefree gold locks (as well as his good-humored expression) that had inadvertently supplanted this image. Automatically, therefore, Selinda found herself returning his kiss with an unreserved passion which astonished them both. Lord Waverly blinked in some surprise, but, quite undaunted, he reached forward to cradle her face in his hands and made as if to repeat that thoroughly satisfying gesture.

Had she not just then heard the telltale creakings of Miss Snypish's rusty stays, Selinda might well have continued in her pursuit of this altogether novel behavior. However, she pulled herself quickly away, grabbed the wayward prayer book, and pushed it to Waverly. "Put it in your pocket quickly, Lord Waverly," she whispered to him with urgent desperation, "and pray don't let that old cat Snypish get a look at it."

Snypish! Waverly thought to himself. Of course! That was the shrew's name. He quickly took the book from Selinda and deposited it deep within the recesses of his greatcoat. He had no sooner complied with this odd request than their relative seclusion beneath the pew was at last interrupted by the distressing appearance of Miss Snypish's pointy features. Simultaneously, a look of such abject terror appeared on Selinda's face that Waverly was moved to automatic chivalry.

"How very good to see you again, my dear Miss Snypish," Waverly whispered companionably, reaching forward to shake her hand in the most affable manner possible. "We have a bit of a problem here, you see. It seems that Lady Selinda's bonnet has caught itself on a splinter. Beastly old benches on the underside, are they not? I shall have to speak to the Bishop about it. Ah, I believe I have got it now. There we go, Lady Selinda," he murmured after several moments of counterfeit attention to her. "Er . . . Do you need some assistance in rising, Miss Snypish?"

"Indeed I do not," she hissed at him. "Lady Selinda, do not imagine that your aunt shall not be told of this episode. Of all the hoydenish spectacles!"

"I do beg your pardon, indeed, Miss Snypish," Waverly continued in an undertone, "but I imagine we must be drawing far more of the congregation's speculation from under this bench than we might if we were to arise one by one and continue quietly through the remainder of the service. Shall we go up in reverse order? Lady Selinda first. There you go. Now I shall follow and then you, Miss Snypish. By the bye," he lied gallantly, "you've become flushed from stooping; indeed you look quite pretty."

Waverly generally did not like resorting to falsehoods and only did so when necessary. He was pleased, therefore, to see that when she finally did emerge, Miss Snypish encountered his eye with a good deal more charity than he had thought her capable of. Perhaps, he mused, some well-placed attention in her quarter (ideally not from him) would serve to draw her venom from Selinda's direction. Again the victim of his own charitable nature, Waverly steeled himself to the distasteful notion of making himself agreeable to the disagreeable.

# *Chapter Six*

A long moment passed as Lucy continued to stare at the ghost. In truth, it had been an age since Lady Sybil had felt the need to retreat behind a fluttering fan, but she did so now with some vigor. Lucy, with admirable fortitude, all things considered, now walked right up to the ghost and delightedly looked her up and down.

"Who are you?" the child finally asked with her characteristic directness.

Lady Sybil looked down at her in some consternation. There was now no doubt that this little girl could see her, but would the creature actually be able to communicate with a ghost? The notion of at last being able to carry on a conversation with someone other than the odd poltergeist roaming through from time to time (Cousin Henry's dreary spirit having at last quitted the house some fifty years previously) was an exciting prospect indeed.

"I am," she ventured at last, "Lady Sybil

Harroweby . . . Er, could you actually *hear* that, child?"

"Oh! Lady Sybil Harroweby!" Lucy breathed in ecstasy. "Why, I knew of course you must be some sort of relation of ours, you look so much like Selinda, but I'd no idea you were Lady Sybil!"

"You have heard of me then?" Lady Sybil inquired with a mixture of confusion and ghostly pride.

"Why, of course! After all, you are the only one in the family who was ever—" Lucy stopped short, suddenly remembering her manners. "Oh, I *am* truly sorry! I did not mean to be indelicate, but I own I quite forgot that my favorite bedtime stories are your life! That is, *were* your life . . . That is . . . Oh, dear!"

"Oh, do go on, child!" the ghost pursued, "I was the only one who was ever what?"

"Why . . . murdered! I really am most sorry, Lady Sybil," Lucy apologized. "I should never have opened my mouth. Indeed, it must have been a dreadful, dreadful blow to find that your own husband—"

"My husband!" Lady Sybil exclaimed, astonished. "Whatever do you mean, child? What on earth could my husband have had to do with the silly business?"

"Well," Lucy continued guardedly, as she wondered about the advisability of launching into an explanation, "it was never proved, of course, but when you were found poisoned and Lord Harroweby suddenly sailed for parts unknown in the company of Viscountess Linfield—"

"Sally Linfield!" the ghost cried out in anguished tones. "Why that false—! That unfaithful—! My dearest friend! Oh, Sally!"

Lucy watched fascinated as the ghost floated back and forth, doing her ethereal best to pace. After decades of having fabricated her anger toward her supposed murderers, it was a new experience for Lady Sybil to feel out and out rage. Sally Linfield had been her bosom friend, or so she had naively thought: so gracious and accommodating, even taking special pains to see that Geoffrey was sufficiently diverted so that Lady Sybil could maintain her own dalliances without fear of discovery and embarrassing scenes. What utter betrayal for Sally to have used those little deceptions for her own disloyal ends! Was there ever an equal to it?

"Lady Sybil?" Lucy interrupted contritely after a time. "I am so very sorry to have brought up such an unpleasant subject. I really do forget myself too often. Even Selinda says so." Lady Sybil had, for a moment, forgotten the child's presence. With a concerted effort of will, she set about calming her rattled vibrations and momentarily turned her attention from this most upsetting revelation.

"So, child," she continued with forced equanimity, "tell me the rest of it. What about my son? Little Roderick, was it not?"

As Lady Sybil uttered her son's name, she felt a momentary twinge of guilt. She had dutifully produced an heir, but he had occupied very little of her time after his birth, the wet nurse being an accommodating soul who had taken the infant to her bosom in more ways than one. Her Ladyship, of course, had visited the nursery on occasion. Why, she could almost swear she had a distinct memory of it. But then again, life had been so very hectic, had it not, and her time so much taken up with social obligations! In any case, the baby had been an exceedingly dull little person who had done nothing but cry, burp, and wet himself. What on earth did people find so attractive about that sort of behavior?

"Well," Lucy shrugged and recited a bit more from the history which had been her personal study ever since she could read the family Bible, "As I recall, Roderick was raised by your cousin, Lord Rookesleigh, and inherited the Harroweby title when he reached his majority. That's all I really know about him except he married my great-grandmother, Miss Marjory Winsdale."

Lady Sybil sighed heavily. Time had certainly flown. Little Roderick! All grown up—and quite likely dead by this time as well! So Roderick was this little creature's great-grandfather! She looked at Lucy with renewed interest. If ever there was a time to find out more about the odd situation which seemed to surround the two sisters, it was now.

"You, too," the ghost began delicately, "would appear to find yourself in odd circumstances. I have been watching you and your sister. Tell me a little about your, er, situation."

At this, Lucy produced a mournful sigh. "Well, madam, I hope you have an interest in sad tales, for ours in certainly one for the novels."

Lady Sybil raised her eyebrows and nodded her

encouragement. Lucy sat down on the carpet, crossed her knees, and began. "Selinda and I were born and raised at the country estate—Darrowdean. You must remember it?" The ghost nodded and leaned forward. "Well, we were perfectly happy, Selinda and I, until about two years ago. Mama and Papa were in London that summer and both of them contracted the typhus. It happened so quickly, it was all over before we could even receive the first letter that told of the illness. Of course, it was shocking news, but Selinda and I were provided for quite well, of course, by the will. We had never been a great deal with our parents, so I am sorry to own it was difficult to miss them much. We were doing quite well, though, when, out of the blue, those three vile toads turned up on the doorstep! It was only six months ago, but I vow it seems like six centuries!

"We had never heard of any living relations," Lucy went on, "and we were just as content to have the estate held in trust until Selinda came of age, but advertisements had been placed in the major newspapers anyway. There wasn't any response, though, until the day Aunt Prudence, Rupert, and that snake Snypish appeared with letters to prove a relationship. Before you know it, Selinda and I had a guardian. What is more," she added in a confiding whisper, "I do not believe that tribe is related to us any more than Guy Fawkes!"

"What about your man of business?" Lady Sybil inquired. "What was his opinion?"

"That is the worst of it," Lucy frowned meditatively. "I have no evidence, but I believe in my heart he is a part of it. It is bad enough that we have no allowance now, we are watched day and night, and I am threatened with boarding school, but we have not a soul we can turn to. And I am much afraid that Selinda will be forced to marry that putrid Rupert. Had we not each been guaranteed a Season in clear legal terms . . ." Just then a look of anxiety flooded across Lucy's small face.

"They're back from services," she whispered, heading at once for the staircase. "I fear I must go now, but we must meet again soon! There is so much to tell you about and so much to ask!"

"Oh dear, child!" the ghost exclaimed, suddenly remembering the conversation she had overheard the night of the ball. "There are several things I must tell you as well! Things concerning Selinda!"

"Promise you will come to our chamber to-night," Lucy whispered hurriedly, "but not while Selinda is there. I am always sent up quite early. Oh dear, I must go down before I am missed. Goodbye, Lady Sybil."

As she turned to go, the child suddenly stopped and a look of consternation suffused her features. "Oh dear! I do beg pardon!" she stammered. "I suppose after all I really should call you Great-great-grandmama!"

Left by herself, the ghost suppressed a shudder. So, she had been murdered by her husband and was a great-great-grandmother besides. Indeed, Lady Sybil reflected, she could not remember having been quite so depressed either in life or death!

# Chapter Seven

Somehow, Selinda was able to survive the remainder of the service in spite of the amused attention she could feel focused on her from all directions. Kneeling, rising, sitting, making responses, she followed Miss Snypish's lead fastidiously, an unreadable expression fixed firmly on her face. Beneath this inscrutable exterior, however, her concentration was divided between two pressing problems: first, how to exit the church without having to face the curiosity of the congregation, and second, how to retrieve her prayer book from Lord Waverly without drawing the attention of Miss Snypish.

It was a very good thing for Selinda's already battered nerves that she did not possess her sister's psychic abilities, for her other difficulties would have been eclipsed by the knowledge that, immediately behind her, Lord Waverly was now occupied in the perusal of the little novel secreted within the innocent covers of her prayer book. The more his

Lordship read of fair Rosamonde's adventures, the more clearly he recalled Selinda's earlier concentration on the book's contents, and the more light-hearted he became. By the end of the first chapter, Waverly was well on the way to falling quite seriously in love with Selinda. By the middle of the second, he had good-naturedly done so. Now, he told himself optimistically, all there was to do was engage the heart of the lady, marry her, and set about refurbishing the nursery. At least, if there were any justice in the universe, it ought to be that simple. Lord Waverly frowned as he remembered Lady Selinda's odd circumstances. He would have to conduct some sort of investigation first. That much was clear.

When the service finally ended, Miss Snypish turned to Selinda and hissed, "On your knees, girl. We shall stay here until the crowd has dispersed. I have no desire to be goggled at on your account."

Selinda gratefully sank onto the kneeler beside her companion, bowed her head, and offered a very thankful prayer indeed, not only for Miss Snypish's decision, but for the privacy afforded by the deep brim of her bonnet. The congregation did take their time leaving, and many stood for an inordinate amount of time chatting with the vicar, but when it became clear that the show was over for the day, they reluctantly turned toward their homes. When the church was finally empty and still, the pair rose and, turning, were quite surprised to see Lord Waverly, still seated with elegant nonchalance in the pew behind them. He stood immediately and smiled.

"Would you do me the honor of accepting my escort, ladies?" he asked civilly. Selinda's heart fluttered at the sight of him, in spite of the ruinous results her earlier meditations on him had occasioned. Moreover, she heaved an inward sigh of relief. Perhaps retrieving her wayward prayer book would not prove so difficult after all. This relief was to be short-lived, however, for Selinda was astounded to see Miss Snypish twist her face into a girlish simper and quite forwardly attach herself to Lord Waverly's extended arm. How in heaven's name would she get her troublesome book back now, she wondered? Then, as she trailed behind the mismatched pair, this concern was supplanted by another of far greater importance: when would she ever have another chance to be with his Lordship?

Oblivious to the splendid fall day, Selinda's thoughts and emotions ranged between chagrin and confusion, irritation and dismay; these became even further disarranged as mysterious snatches of the conversation between Miss Snypish and Lord Waverly drifted back.

"I feel most fortunate, my dear Miss Snypish, to have this opportunity for some private words with you," Waverly began. "I own, this had been my aim today, but I had no reason to hope I might accomplish it."

Miss Snypish's withered heart began to beat erratically. She had always dreamed that the very obvious good sense which shone from her face would someday attract a man in need of that sterling quality, but she had begun of late to lose hope. She was now chagrined to find that her usually quick tongue seemed to have deserted her, for she could think of nothing whatsoever to say. Fortunately, Waverly took her silence for the invitation it was and plunged forward into verbal improvisation.

"You surely cannot have been insensible to the degree of interest your presence at last night's ball inspired," he lied blithely. "You must have been aware of so many longing glances cast in your direction."

Miss Snypish's jaw dropped almost to her chest, but still she could not reply. She only hoped that his Lordship would construe her stunned silence as eloquent rather than asinine.

Waverly, floundering about in a morass of half-formed ideas, went on desperately, "I know my conduct must seem precipitate, but I hope you do not think me overly bold to speak to you in this manner."

"Oh, no," she finally managed to sputter. "Indeed, I think no such thing. Pray continue, your Lordship."

"I do not speak for myself, you understand," Waverly put in quickly, his sense of self-preservation forcing its way through the tangle of invention. With it came a sudden and brilliant inspiration. "It is my cousin, the Marquess of Bastion. He is a timid fellow, you see. Painfully so. He gazed at you from afar last night and was struck with your classic profile, your glance of keen intelligence. Alas, he could not find either the courage or opportunity to approach you. He begged me to find a way of making himself known to you. Can you take pity on the poor wretch?"

Miss Snypish was momentarily disappointed: Lord Waverly was the sort of fellow who looked like he needed a firm hand and her pulse had indeed fluttered at the prospect. Nevertheless, it took only a heartbeat for her interest to transfer from the nobleman by her side to his unsuspecting cousin. "Your cousin," she responded meditatively. "A marquess, you say?"

"Pray do not hold it against him, Miss Snypish. It is, after all, just a title. Say you will meet him." In the uncomfortable silence that followed, Waverly wondered if he hadn't poured it on a bit too thick.

Finally, Miss Snypish answered. "There may be some difficulty, your Lordship. My position as companion to Lady Selinda's aunt is quite arduous. Moreover, my duties often extend to playing duenna as well. As you can tell from today's little performance, *those* duties are not to be sneezed at either. However, I have no doubt that something may be contrived. Could you send a footman tomorrow to carry a message?"

Lord Waverly bowed in response. As the two fell into the respective silence of their own meditations, Selinda's spirits drooped lower and lower. She had not overheard all, by any means; however, it was enough to realize that Lord Waverly's attention was not focused on her but on the offensive Miss Snypish. Her good sense told her that Lord Waverly was generously deflecting the companion's wrath, but life had been so odd lately, one wondered. Could a penchant for older, unattractive women be the basis for the remarks she had heard last night about his Lordship's eccentricities? She sincerely hoped not. The idyllic moment beneath the pew was one she would always cherish, but she hardly dared to hope for more. Indeed, the gentleman had not so much as looked at her since leaving the church. Now, as she regarded Miss Snypish's angular form beside Lord Waverly's elegant one, she could not help but think the world had gone quite mad and nothing would ever be as it ought again.

When his Lordship left the ladies at the doorstep, Miss Snypish looked decidedly flushed, and Selinda steeled herself for the repercussions from which she felt certain Waverly's presence had shielded her. Immediately on their entry, however, Miss Snypish, her eyes darting back and forth in a most underhanded manner, pulled Selinda aside and whispered, "That Lord Waverly seems to be quite a gentlemanly sort and I would not for anything encourage your aunt's prying in this matter. I believe we shall keep the story of this morning's commotion to ourselves."

"As you wish, Miss Snypish," Selinda returned, mightily relieved, but her curiosity piqued.

"One more thing, your Ladyship," Miss Snypish went on hurriedly after some slight hesitation. "I have a notion this old gray sarcenet gown does not become me as well as it might. What would you say to something a little gayer . . . chartreuse, for example?"

Selinda's eyebrows rose just a fraction at the thought of this noxious prospect. It seemed altogether unlikely, but the puritanical Miss Snypish must have formed a sudden *tendre* for Lord Waverly as well. What else would explain this severe person's sudden interest in apparel, heretofore condemned as foolish frippery?

"Why, I should have to see you in it, Miss Snypish," she ventured cautiously, "but I daresay a little change might be to your advantage." Thinking quickly, Selinda pursued this sudden but odd alliance a bit further, "Indeed, if we could but find a way to drive out tomorrow afternoon, we might visit my late mother's modiste and try some swatches of color against your complexion."

Miss Snypish had nodded slowly. "That might be managed. Pray then, be sure to tell your aunt how pale she looks when next you see her and depend on me to contrive the rest." With that, she turned abruptly and left Selinda to ponder the morning's bizarre twists and turns.

When she finally achieved the refuge of her chamber, Selinda discovered Lucy sitting at the desk, busily employed in making up a list. Had her own thoughts and emotions not been so tousled, she would have noted that her ordinarily staid little sister looked very much like the cat who swallowed the canary.

"Good morning, Selinda," Lucy greeted with a gay smile. "How was the service? I must say you do not look terribly pious for all the time you have no doubt spent at the church pew."

At that remark, Selinda's thoughts suddenly returned to the time spent *under* the church pew. Recollections of that encounter, both idyllic and idiotic, caused a small worry line to form between her eyebrows. What on earth must Lord Waverly have thought of her, not only accepting his kiss but returning it with such embarrassing vigor? And what was he doing kissing her if he meant to pay such marked attentions to Miss Snypish? Perhaps what was said about men was true: anything in a skirt! And yet, she mused, her cheeks warming at the memory, the kiss really had been very nice, hadn't it?

Enough of that, she told herself sternly after several moments of self-indulgent reminiscence. Such notions! She really ought to have fainted from the effrontery of his bold action. Certainly, she should not have returned the salute. Oh, it was all the fault of that senseless novel, she raged inwardly. If only she had not been envisioning Lord Waverly as the hero of that particular tale she surely would have had some self-control!

Lord Waverly was, of course, the handsomest man whose acquaintance she'd made on the previous night. It was more than that, though; he was also the only gentleman present who'd spoken to her with directness and interest. The other conversations, however polite, had been mere strings of transparent flattery and none-too-subtle angling for information as to the size of her fortune. Lord Waverly had seemed so different from the rest. Little wonder he'd found a place in her overactive imagination. Selinda sighed heavily. Yes, the book had begun it and her fanciful nature had jumped on board, but she had to admit it was her dratted romantic heart that settled the matter.

71

She only prayed his Lordship could keep his own counsel!

"Selinda? Selinda, I've been talking to you!"

"I'm sorry, Lucy. My mind is in the clouds today. What is it?"

"I have been wondering about our family history. How long has it been since our family actually lived in Harroweby House?"

Selinda thought for a moment. "At least a hundred years, I should think. Perhaps more."

"It really could be a lovely place. Why did they leave?"

"Unhappy connections, I imagine. You've heard the story of Lady Sybil often enough. Then, of course, there was rumor that the house was haunted. But that's just silliness—I hope you don't go worrying yourself about it."

"Of course not," Lucy replied with an odd smile. "I should be very silly indeed!"

Their conversation was interrupted at that moment by the entrance of the upstairs maid, Dorcas. "Beg pardon, your Ladyship," she began, curtseying nervously, "but your cousin has awoke quite unwell and begs you come to his chamber and read to him."

"To his chamber!" Selinda sputtered, clearly horrified.

"I shall come with you, Selinda," Lucy volunteered, quickly jumping to her feet.

"Beg pardon, your Ladyship," Dorcas went on, not looking directly at either girl. "Mr. Rupert were most plain. He said Lady Selinda *only*."

"Of all the—" Lucy began darkly.

72

"Hush, Lucy," Selinda preempted her. She cast about momentarily for an excuse, any excuse, to save her from an encounter fraught with such impropriety, but could think of nothing. Dorcas stood waiting expectantly. Selinda sighed helplessly. "Rupert is our cousin, after all, and a clergyman besides. I suppose there is really nothing untoward . . ."

"Nothing untoward!" Lucy muttered to herself as she watched her sister exit.

Selinda made her way ruefully to the other wing of the house, wondering with alarm what other complications she must negotiate before the day was through. It was, she knew quite well, altogether improper to visit her cousin's chamber, in spite of her reassurances to Lucy. If she refused, however, she knew from sad experience that Rupert or his mother would find a way of making Lucy suffer. The conniving pair had discovered early on that any threat to Lucy's well-being was a sure route to guaranteeing Selinda's docility.

Finding herself at length in the east wing, she hesitated for a moment before going on. In her heart she knew that Rupert's intentions, however well-cloaked in the language of piety, were very black indeed. Not for the first time, she felt the chilling absence of friends and protectors. Feeling very much like a wobbly little lamb entering a wolf's den, she knocked lightly at her cousin's door. She left it well ajar as she took a deep breath and ventured into the dim recesses.

Rupert's chamber was swathed in purple velvet hangings and reeked of the strong scent in which he daily doused himself, forbearing the dangers of a bath except at yearly intervals. Deep within the curtained cavern of a large canopy bed, his nasal voice issued in a pitiful wail, "Are you come at last, Selinda? I have been languishing here this age."

"Indeed, Cousin," she returned with forced briskness which belied her spirits, "your lot is very hard. You wished me to read to you?"

"You must come closer," he moaned. "I cannot hear you, my dear."

Repressing images of herself in a red riding hood, Selinda gingerly advanced a step or two and cast about for a candle. The chamber's windows were still heavily curtained against the brilliance of the day and very little light from the hallway penetrated the room. Selinda was loath to proceed further into the semidarkness without some clue as to what the shadows held for her. Memories of Rupert's odious advances lingered in every shadow. His boldness after the ball last night had merely been the most recent incident in an escalating series.

"Heavens, Cousin," she ventured nervously, "However am I to read to you in this darkness? I vow I can hardly see to put one foot before the other. Have you not a candle nearby?"

Rupert merely moaned again, reminding Selinda more of a calf with colic than anything else. Well, she thought to herself with a shrug, surely there must be some sort of lamp or candle on the bedside table. She stepped slowly forward through the gloom until at length she was quite close to her cousin's bed. Fumbling about on the nightstand, she felt numerous bottles of medication, a basin and pitcher, several wadded handkerchiefs, a vial of salts, various snuffboxes, but no candle. This would never do.

Selinda had just decided to go to the window to draw the curtains when her arm was suddenly grasped and she found herself pulled precipitously down into the depths of Rupert's bed. Caught abruptly off balance, Selinda was quite unable to prevent herself from landing in an ungainly heap directly on top of her cousin's generous midsection with a resounding plop.

Rupert immediately let forth a stifled gasp, sounding not unlike a despondent tea kettle, but he did not loosen his hold on her in the least. As Selinda felt herself being pulled inexorably towards his bulk, she realized she was in a struggle, not for life or death, but for a life worth living or a fate worse than death. As Selinda labored to right herself, she could feel the moist heat of his whisper on the back of her neck, "Here, let me help you, little cousin." Then, as he pretended to support her back, he allowed his other hand to stray to her bosom.

Selinda, beside herself with outrage, could only flail about for she dared not cry out: to raise the house would only bring witnesses to this wretched situation and guarantee beyond all salvation a hastily arranged wedding. Should that monstrous disaster come about, her own fate and that of her little sister would be immediately sealed. Silently, therefore, she struggled on, gritting her teeth, all the while shuddering against the steady progress being made towards her demise.

After several moments of strained concentration, Rupert had succeeded in undoing most of Selinda's tapes and buttons. Silently he cursed his mother's unfortunate strictures on his cousin's dress. He was so close to his mark, but Selinda's squirming, enticing as it was, hindered his progress till he was ready to scream with frustration and annoyance. Finally, another button gave way and he had just begun to attack the last when he felt himself suddenly doused with a shocking cascade of ice-cold water. Sputtering with astonishment, he momentarily loosed his hold, and Selinda promptly seized this opportunity to spring from the bed and run from the room, clutching her gown about her as best she could.

Rupert shuddered and shook himself violently. How on earth, he wondered with bad-tempered incredulity, had the little vixen managed to reach the pitcher? He was sure she could not have touched it with her hands. She must have hooked the handle with a foot—Gads! The girl must be a contortionist! Shuddering with rage and cold, he scowled into the darkness.

The flirtations in which Rupert had jealously watched his luscious cousin engage on the previous night had seriously disarranged his sleep. In the fitful predawn hours he had, therefore, plotted to maneuver the unsuspecting girl into his bed for the sake of a quick compromise of her virtue and appropriation of her fortune, neatly putting her out of the way of other rivals. Having the wind knocked out of him and receiving an unseasonal ablution, however, was not a part of that plan.

Perhaps, he reflected with a damp shudder, he should have enlisted his mother's aid in this scheme. Certainly, if she could have been on hand to surprise them in the midst of entanglement, he would have been on his way in the morning to post the banns. But no, he reconsidered grimly, it was best to keep the old harridan at arm's length. She was getting altogether too managing these days.

After all, if their plan worked, the estate would fall to him as Selinda's husband. Then his mother could be sent to Bridewell for aught he cared. In fact, that might be just the ticket, he told himself as he began to towel his person meditatively.

Yes, he smiled, the Snipe could be bought off and sent on her way, Mater committed to a silent keeper with a stout truncheon, and a few months in a clammy climate would consign that brat Lucy to consumption. Her portion would fall to Selinda and, thence, to him. Moreover, there could be no impediments to his doing exactly what he liked with his captivating but disdainful cousin. He pulled a packet from under his mattress, wrapped himself in a blanket, and crossed to the window. Pulling back the curtain, he leered at a dog-eared set of French postcards depicting in graphically detailed etchings several quite interesting activities for which he had lately begun to cherish a sweltering fondness. Ah, Selinda, he sighed inwardly, what times we shall have. Then he settled himself into a chair and began to refine his plans.

## Chapter Eight

As soon as her sister had disappeared down the
hall to Rupert's chamber, Lucy made her own
rapid departure toward the opposite wing of
Harroweby House. If Lady Sybil Harroweby were
indeed "the lady who looks after us," Lucy
reasoned, there seemed to be no time like the
present for her to begin. In a few moments, she
reached the dim gallery where the shade of Lady
Sybil still hovered in a brown study, and apprised
her of the danger in which she felt certain her sister
Selinda would soon find herself. The ghost,
riveted by the child's breathless communication,
had wasted no time but dematerialized forthwith,
and Lucy spent several moments pacing wretchedly
and thinking excessively dark thoughts until her
ghostly relation reappeared. When she did so, the
poor spirit was a good ten shades paler (and
markedly more transparent) than she had been
before her exit.

"Whatever has happened?" Lucy cried, running

up to the languishing apparition.

Lady Sybil settled herself weakly and lifted a preemptory finger. For the next several minutes Lucy could only look on miserably in the pitiful silence, biting her already tortured fingernails, until the ghost began to regain her diaphanous self.

"Something really must be done soon," Lady Sybil sighed weakly. "I am feeling more myself now, but I am very much afraid that I shall not often be equal to this sort of exertion."

Lucy had for some moments been torn in her distress between Selinda's horrid plight and the spirit's obviously fragile condition. Now, somewhat relieved on at least one score, she leaned forward eagerly to hear the ghost's account of the shocking scene which had just been played in Rupert's chamber. Lady Sybil, in the spirit of newfound discretion (and to her eternal credit), rendered a somewhat edited version of the scene she had just witnessed, but Lucy, with her uncanny insight, seized immediately on the true nature of the encounter.

"Maggoty cad! So the scoundrel means to ruin her, does he?" the child muttered, her eyes narrowing dangerously. "I should have seen how it would be! I should have known he would be up to some foul trick or other, but this is beyond anything! Of course, he must have guessed she would have the likes of him no honest way, but I did not dream he would act so soon. How were you able to stop him, Great-great-grandmama?"

Lucy's ancient but vain relation shuddered at

being thus titled and raised a repressive eyebrow. "*Lady Sybil* will do quite well, child. Fortunately," she went on, "the scoundrel's ewer was quite full of water, so I doused him; that is, I am afraid that both of them received a thorough watering. I have never before attempted anything quite so heavy. I can only assume my powers were enhanced by my rage. It is a fortuitous thing for our purposes, though, that he had not yet washed himself."

"Nor would he have been likely to have done so for an age or so," Lucy remarked with an exceedingly ill-humored grimace. "You may count your blessings, Lady Sybil, that you are not possessed of a sense of smell. Pungent as a polecat is our Rupert."

"Be that as it may," the ghost went on with a determined sigh, "the effort is not one I could repeat very soon. My powers are quite limited, and I very much fear it will take more than a mere wetting to foil your cousin's plans next time—"

"Next time!" Lucy interrupted with a gasp.

Lady Sybil assumed a world-weary air. "There is *always* a next time, child, particularly with that rotter's ilk. Moreover," she continued grimly, shuddering as she remembered Rupert's flushed visage as he studied his lurid postcards (which had shocked even her seasoned sensibilities), "he has plans. Despicable plans. As I say, child, my capabilities are decidedly scant and even this minimal amount of exertion has rendered me very nearly unsubstantial. I hate to even think it, but if my aim had missed its mark, I should have been powerless to do further till I recovered and by then it might well have been too late."

"Oh, dear," Lucy cried in sad exasperation. "Everything might have been lost before we had even begun to fight. Whatever shall we do?"

"Well, my dear," Lady Sybil announced finally with a determined smile, "we shall just have to take stock of the weapons we have at hand. I do not believe we have a great deal of time, but together we shall contrive some sort of plan, never you fear, child."

Somewhat comforted, Lucy settled herself to the task at hand. "First of all, just what are your powers? What can you do besides douse dastards?"

Lady Sybil paused for a moment trying to decide, after all those years, just which of her talents had been acquired only after she had achieved her ghostly state. "Well," she began slowly, "I can think myself places . . ."

"How do you mean?"

"Well, I just envision the drawing room or the library, for example, and—poof—there I am." As she spoke these words, she suddenly disappeared from Lucy's sight and reappeared almost as quickly. Looking a trifle embarrassed, the ghost went on, "I see I shall have to be more careful in future."

"Can you think yourself anywhere at all?" Lucy asked.

"Oh no, only within this house or the surrounding gardens, unless there are special circumstances. For example, if something I owned during my lifetime is taken out of the house for some reason or other, I am free to follow it."

"Capital!" Lucy exclaimed. "That's one problem solved."

"How so?" the ghost inquired. Sometimes it seemed the child's rapid reasoning far outpaced her own, although Lady Sybil knew quite well that, in life, she had been more renowned for her beauty than her intellect.

"Why, we are restricted, Selinda and I. We cannot stir without being watched, you know, so it's near enough impossible for us to confirm any of our suspicions. But *you* might venture out where we may not, to Mr. Basham's, say,—he's our man of business—and see what sort of information you might puzzle out. One way or the other," she concluded with an assured nod, "knowing is better than not knowing, I always say."

In light of recent revelations concerning the authors of her demise, Lady Sybil was hard-pressed to agree. Moreover, the very thought of spending who knew what amount of time within the grimy recesses of a solicitor's office seemed deadly dull to the fun-loving spirit. However, she kept these sentiments to herself for the moment.

"What else can you do?" Lucy prodded.

The ghost concentrated for several more moments. Then her face was lit with a thoughtful smile. "There are a few minor accomplishments," she admitted modestly, "such as sending a chill through a room if I happen to be in bad temper. All ghosts, of course, can emit the scent of sandalwood, although I own I have never found that skill terribly useful. However, I do have one rather interesting talent which may well be of particular use to us."

Lucy looked at her expectantly.

"I can tamper with dreams," she said with a decidedly mischievous smile.

Upon regaining her chamber, Selinda was relieved to find that Lucy was no longer there. To deal with her sister's understandable curiosity and concern was more than her rattled resources were equal to for the moment. As she stripped off her soaking garments, she wondered in dazed abstraction whether her mental or physical demeanor were the most disheveled: certainly both had sustained an icy shock. Suddenly she froze, mid-motion, her sodden skirts about her ankles. Where, in heaven's name, had the watery cascade come from?

She recalled with an anguished certainty that both her own and Rupert's hands had been busily engaged. Neither of them had any means of reaching the ewer. There was only one explanation and an appalling one at that: Lucy must have silently followed her to Rupert's chamber and been a witness to the whole disgusting scene. Selinda buried her face in her hands as she confronted this sorry conclusion. Indeed, there was no other accounting for her sudden salvation. Lucy *must* have emptied the pitcher on them. No wonder the child was not in the chamber: she could not face her sister's disgrace. With this dreadful realization, Selinda gave way at last to the teary floodwaters that had been building behind her eyes for some hours now, and she collapsed before the fireplace in a shuddering heap of soggy garments and heartfelt sobs.

Selinda continued in this manner for some minutes until at last her sense of helplessness began to alter and reemerge with equal vigor under the guise of a grim and studied rage. Her own sorrows she had long since determined she could and must bear, but that her innocent little sister should share the burden was beyond enough. Something must be done. But what?

Selinda sat up shivering and hugged her knees to her chest. According to the strictures of her parents' will, she would not gain her independence for still another three years. The events of the last several hours proved beyond any doubt that the likelihood of her emerging from her guardianship with anything like independence was not to be thought of. Not unless she were able to somehow take matters into her own hands. Selinda sighed and frowned as she rejected one senseless scheme after another. The options for independence were simply nonexistent as long as such horrid guardians held the reins of her fate.

Marriage was the only deliverance Selinda could imagine, but she hardly knew how she might bring about even so much as a small flirtation, so closely watched as she was. True, Miss Snypish's apparent change of attitude promised some relief, but such a person was hardly to be counted upon. Even taking into account cooperation from that unlikely quarter, the amount of time necessary to bring about even a whirlwind courtship would, in all likelihood, not be available to her. It was appallingly clear that Rupert had decided to—

Suddenly, Selinda sat upright. The solution was quite simple: a compromise of her virtue was indeed the answer. All she must do was to find a good-natured, biddable gentleman, one on whom she could depend to be kind to herself and Lucy, and force him to marry her. Except for his unaccountable penchant for spinsterish persons, Lord Waverly would do admirably. And, after all, that peculiarity made no odds at all when compared with the loathsome propensities of her degenerate cousin. Moreover, his Lordship's attentions, however short-lived, had been anything but odious. Indeed, it seemed quite possible that, in spite of his idiosyncrasies, she should be able to love him before too long. Perhaps, Selinda mused, she already did.

True, she had not known Lord Waverly for very long, but she knew of similar incidents of instant amour: Valeria had succumbed immediately to the flashing eyes of Rothwell in *The Abducted Heart*, and Melisande in *The Rake's Reform* had surrendered her heart at her first glimpse of Blackthorne's miniature. So, if her budding attachment was indeed love, she reasoned, Lord Waverly was hers by rights and she would have him.

Selinda smiled, sniffed, and began to feel much better as she began to plot a mental framework for his Lordship's seduction. She wasn't quite certain how it all worked, but she had heard that a proper

85

lady was never seen without her gloves. Bare hands, she had often been cautioned, gave gentlemen all sorts of ideas. That seemed a logical place to start.

For his part, Lord Waverly was also busily engaged in plans for bringing about a satisfactory conclusion to his romantic ambitions. After a nap and a change of costume, he presented himself at the rooms of his cousin, Lord Bastion, just as that person was beginning to stir from his bed for the first time that day.

"Bastion, old fellow!" he called energetically as he strode noisily into the bedchamber and threw open the heavy curtains with a ruthless flourish. "Whatever are you about—sleeping away like an overfed kitchen cat on this glorious day!"

Bastion frowned darkly and immediately pulled the covers up over his bleary eyes. The marquess had also enjoyed a frightfully late night, but his head, regrettably, was a good deal more susceptible to the ravages of brandy than was his cousin's. In fact, it felt as if some group of badly behaved children had used his noddle in a game of bilbocatch during the night. Survival instinct, however, won out over anguish and indignation, and he forbore to voice the crushing oath which rose automatically to his lips. Waverly, curse the luck, held the pursestrings.

"Up and about, Bastion," his Lordship commanded heartily, pulling the covers from the foot of the bed and exposing his cousin's bare feet to the brisk fall air, "or would you rather I departed without rescuing your poor fortune from the ravages it has lately undergone?"

At this odd question, the marquess peeped slowly from under the eiderdown and studied his cousin's face with deep suspicion: to begin with, it was highly uncharacteristic for Waverly to be so cheerful, nay, downright cordial, in his cousin's presence. They had never in their lives gotten on. Moreover, the marquess's admittedly reckless spending habits had invariably met with little patience and no sympathy from his Lordship. That gentleman had never once had the decency to look on temporary runs of bad luck with anything like charity. There was something not quite right about all of this.

"Now, then, that's much better," Waverly approved as he watched his cousin's all-too-obvious ruminations march across his bleary visage. Seating himself on the edge of the bed, Waverly went on, "Coffee should be here shortly, and after you have downed a pot or two, we can begin to discuss the details."

"Details?" Bastion queried warily. As he studied his cousin's sphinxlike expression, he was not at all certain that he wanted to know to what his cousin referred.

Waverly laughed briefly. "Indeed, Cousin, a brilliant idea came to me during the night. I own that I have, from time to time, been somewhat troubled by your various escapades, unpaid notes, brushes with unreasonable husbands and papas, but you hit on an ingenious solution to your difficulties at last night's gathering and I had not the wit to see it."

Bastion knit his brows and cast back over what he could recall about the previous evening. He mainly recalled downing a good deal of brandy at his club. "I haven't the first clue what you are talking about," he pronounced flatly.

"Of course you have not, sapskull!" Waverly rejoined, ruffling his cousin's hair in a manner calculated to annoy, "for you've even less wit than I!"

"Well?" Bastion prompted impatiently, ignoring the insult. "Pray, just what is your solution to my dissolution?"

"A wife!" Waverly pronounced triumphantly.

Here a weighty pause intervened. "I beg your pardon?" Bastion finally ventured with a dumbfounded expression. "Did I hear you aright? A wife?"

"Ex-act-ly!" Waverly smiled triumphantly as a serving man entered with a coffee service. Taking it from him, Waverly poured out two cups and set one into his cousin's hands. "I am afraid I did you a very great disservice last night, Bastion. You solicited from me an introduction to an eligible young lady and I declined to make you known to her. I have now reconsidered the matter. In fact, I believe a steady woman of unimpeachable character and gentle background must be the very thing to set your fortunes straight."

The dim light of understanding slowly dawned in Bastion's eyes. Now his memory of the previous evening came rushing back to him, including his wager with Slaverington. What a paperskull his cousin was! That is, if he was reading him correctly.

"So," the marquess ventured carefully, "am I to understand that you will actually arrange for me to meet Lady Selinda?"

"That is a part of my plan," Waverly admitted, although he had not the least intention of revealing the whole of it to his cousin. "However," he went on slowly, "there are some considerable impediments involved, as you might well imagine."

"Ah, yes," Bastion sighed with disheartened recollection, "the Gorgons!"

"Just as you say, the Gorgons," Waverly confirmed, "but I believe I have found an inroad if you will but trust me implicitly and do exactly as I say."

# *Chapter Nine*

The next day, Lucy found herself unaccountably at her leisure, unsupervised and, hence, unvexed. Her sister and Miss Snypish had left together on an errand immediately after breakfast, and Aunt Prudence and Rupert had closeted themselves in another part of the house all morning with strict orders that they not be disturbed on any pretext. That was an order which Lucy felt most inclined to obey. She had seen no sign of Lady Sybil since their conference on the previous afternoon. At that time, they had both determined to gather as much information as they might by whatever means at their disposal in order to form some sort of plan.

Lucy's familiarity with her own genealogy was limited to such remote history as constituted interesting tales and legends, and she now attempted to discover more practical information. She had hoped to make an investigation into the various branches of the family which might currently survive in hopes of determining the sort of relationship (if any) to which Aunt Prudence might hold claim. Surprisingly, however, she could find no copy of the family chronicles in the library. Moreover, one page of records in the family bible appeared to have been neatly removed.

"Blast it!" she muttered, then quickly clapped her hands over her mouth. She really would have to watch her language. Selinda, she knew, would have been sorry to have heard such an oath from her little sister's lips, and her guardians would have used the blunder as an excuse for one of their odious punishments. With a concerted effort of will, Lucy suppressed her vexation and, perching in the morning room's sunny windowseat, turned her energies to listing the facts as she knew them:

1) Mama and Papa never made mention of any relations (note: may not have been on visiting terms with Rupert and Aunt P. Understandable.).

2) Rupert and Aunt P. did not claim ties until after advertisement had been posted (note: if not on visiting terms, might not have been aware until then).

3) Rupert and Aunt P. made difficulties about arrangements in London (note: they are of the sort to make difficulties, regardless).

4) Pinch-penny ways—may be funneling funds to their own coffers.

Lucy set down her pen and frowned. All she had were her suspicions. It was true that Aunt Prudence and Rupert were unspeakably vile, but that, in and of itself, was not evidence of wrong-doing. It was further clear that Rupert had plans to gain access to their entire fortune by any means, however contemptible, but even Lucy, for all her youth, knew that his was not an uncommon scheme. In addition to this frustrating line of reasoning, her glimpses of second sight, while more frequent, were proving more annoying than helpful. Tantalizing clues and vague images wove themselves about her waking and sleeping hours. The air fairly buzzed with plotting and planning, but she found it impossible to sort through the tangled web. Nevertheless, she sighed resignedly, pressed her fingers to her temples, and tried to concentrate.

Lady Sybil, on the other hand, was finding few impediments to her investigations that morning. She had watched with amusement as Rupert shut the doors to the red saloon, bolted them securely, pushed a settee against them for good measure, and, finally, pulled the curtains shut. These precautions notwithstanding, the pair had drawn their chairs within a hairsbreadth of each other and spoke in such confidential whispers that the ghost was forced to perch invisibly on Rupert's generous lap in order to hear their conversation.

"Do stop twitching, Rupert," his mother admonished. "You are setting my nerves all ajangle."

"I cannot help it, Mater," he told her in hollow tones. "I have the most shivery feeling. Like a goose walked over my grave."

His mother looked at him narrowly. His manner had been very odd lately. "Well, my own," she told him, "this shan't take long. Then you must rest again. I only hope you have not taken the ague. There are a number of things we must speak of, however, and time grows short."

"What a good thing it was that the Snipe was so easily got rid of this morning," Rupert began. "That viper knows too much already."

"Trust me, my own," his mother returned with a sage nod, "her usefulness to us is limited and quickly drawing to a close. Believe me, she shall not get more than the scraps she deserves. The same goes for that insect Basham. Now mark me, Rupert: another week and we shall have completed the sale of Darrowdean. We have already built up quite a considerable fortune, you know, by merely selling off oddments here and there. Soon, we shall be able to make off with a fine nest egg, with or without the remainder of the chit's fortune. I have given the matter some considerable thought of late, and I am not at all convinced that she is quite the thing for you, my sweeting."

At this, Rupert's eyes narrowed to angry slits in his corpulent face. "I do not mean to discuss this item, Mater," he spat. "I have taken a fancy for her and I shall have her, one way or another."

"At least," his mother allowed, "you have the sense to see that there is more than *one* way of having her at your disposal."

Refusing to be satisfied with this odious insinuation, Rupert continued in a frosty tone, "I will not brook interference, Mater. I shall have her as my wife in our own establishment. It is bad enough one such as I must worry about rivals but to endure your fiddling about is not to be borne. That wretched ball was certainly a nodcock idea. I did not at all relish the attentions I witnessed being paid to her, especially by that odious Lord Waverly. I thought you promised only dotards and rakes would take notice of her."

"But, my sugar plum," his mother protested, shocked at such rebellion from her darling, "you know that giving the girl her season provided us an opportunity to conduct our sale of Darrowdean without interference, and the ball gave us a way of ruining her chances of taking. I was at great pains to see that the worst debauchees and eccentrics in society—and mind you, his Lordship is accounted one of the latter—were present in great numbers, as well as a number of nobodies and upstarts. It was an ill-assorted group, and you will remark there have been but few cards and no callers at all. She could not possibly have taken. Regardless what plans you may have in mind for the little baggage, I doubt that any shall take notice of her situation or lift a finger if they do. I have made sure that she is quite, quite friendless."

"Do let us hope so. Trust me, I am not about to countenance meddling from anyone in this affair. And, should we be discovered, I have no intention of assuming any blame. Gaol may be old home to you, Mater," he sneered unkindly, "but I do not fancy changing my residence in that manner."

"Have a care, Rupert! You know well enough I have forbid you to speak of such things," his mother hissed viciously, for once abandoning the honeyed terms in which she usually addressed her darling. She looked at him with an appraising squint before continuing coldly, "I would not be so high in the instep if I were you. You are no more a clergyman than I am a gentlewoman. It would not be at all wise were you to forget the necessity of my goodwill. And as for prison, do not forget that you missed being born in that hole by mere days. There is some good fortune in all things and you will recall that my first acquaintance with our Mr. Basham, Shambeigh as he was called in those days, took place within those same prison walls. I have done enough suffering for both of us, but mean to profit by it now. If you but heed me in all things, there should be no reason for this plan to fail."

During this lecture, Rupert took pains to assume the look (if not the spirit) of chastened repentance for his ill-judged remarks. He had witnessed the results of his mother's cold anger before this, but never had it been directed at him until now. It was not a pleasant experience. When his mother had finished speaking, he cocked his head at her and pasted a winning smile on his pudgy face, a maneuver which, in the past, had never failed to win her forgiveness. She stared back at him now, however, with a steely expression. Chilled, he went on in a placatory tone, "How fortunate it was that you had the wit to see past that rogue Basham's wig and paint. When you called to him using his true name, I vow I thought he would swallow his tongue, he started so. The very idea of a convicted forger passing as a respected solicitor! It makes me laugh! Do you think we can rely on him, though?"

"He can risk exposure even less than we. After all," she smiled smugly, "it was he who suggested and promoted this scheme, albeit to save himself from the blackmail I hinted at. I think he has no choice but to honor our compact. Now to business, Rupert. You and I must take ourselves to the country in two day's time to settle matters at Darrowdean. Snypish shall have orders that the chits are not to stir a foot outside."

"And why doesn't Selinda come with us? I am not easy leaving her here."

Rupert's mother regarded him with an icy glint.

"All right, then, it will be but a few days, I suppose. But what shall we do about visitors?" he asked agitatedly. "I do not want them having any visitors."

"There is but little fear of that; however, I shall have it put about that we are all under quarantine here. Snypish, you must own, looks admirably like a charnel house attendant for all her superior airs."

"Have you thought how we shall be rid of that one? I wager the Snipe's as tenacious as a pit bull when it comes to money matters. Gads," he shuddered in sudden recollection, "I had the most beastly dream about her last night! I am sure it was a sign of some sort, but I wonder what it can mean?" Here Lady Sybil smiled to herself. It had just been a practice run, sending that dream, but she was gratified to hear she had not lost her old touch.

"Never fear, Rupert," his mother assured him. "There shall be no trouble from that quarter.

When my arrangements have been made final, I shall tell you all. But mark me: when we return from Darrowdean, you must be prepared to depart again at a moment's notice."

Rupert did not in the least relish his mother's sudden secrecy anymore than her hints that Selinda was not to be his in more than a cursory way. She had been used to sharing all of her schemes with him till lately. Why, she was as cagey as a cat. It was an excessively good thing, he decided, that he had already begun planning his own alternate arrangements.

After the frustration of her fruitless morning's endeavor, Lucy was gratified to recognize at last the airy form of Lady Sybil taking shape before her. As the ghost's features clarified, Lucy was intrigued to see thereon a look of decided perplexity.

"Well, Lucy," Lady Sybil sighed, "I am afraid you and your sister have landed yourselves quite in the middle of a nest of vipers and no mistake! I never saw the like for corruption and iniquity! And not only are these creatures the veriest frauds as you so rightly suspected, but it would also appear that they are making every attempt to dupe each other as wickedly as they are you! Honor among thieves, indeed!"

Lucy hugged herself, exulting inwardly at finding her instincts vindicated. There was really hardly anything, she decided, so nice as being right. Then, sobering abruptly as she remembered their predicament, she urged the ghost to explain herself.

"It is difficult to know where to begin," Lady Sybil frowned with exasperation, "so much appears to have been misrepresented and the gaps in the story have by no means been filled in."

"Then begin anywhere you like," Lucy told her complacently, "and then we can attempt to piece it all together."

By the time Lucy had unraveled Lady Sybil's narrative, however, she was very nearly cross-eyed with confusion. "So," the child said at length, knitting her brows, "Rupert is neither a clergyman nor our cousin, Aunt Prudence is not our aunt, and Mr. Basham is not Mr. Basham. I declare, I begin to wonder if *I* am who I think."

"Well," the ghost returned philosophically, "at least Miss Snypish appears to be who she claims, although her complicity in this wretched matter is not altogether plain. It is clear, however, that we shall have but little time to get matters into hand if we are ever to save Darrowdean. It will be difficult to retrieve once its sale has been finalized."

"What?" cried Lucy, aghast.

"Did I not mention that part?" the ghost asked with a small shrug. "I am sorry, child, but my poor head is all abuzz with plots and counterplots, and I have always been a sorry goosecap when it comes to details. Yes, the transaction will apparently take place at the end of the week. But at least you and Selinda will have some time to yourselves, for the pair will be leaving for the country to oversee the exchange in a day or two. All you will have to do is find a way to evade that Snypish creature. Now, I believe I shall take myself belowstairs and see if I can learn anything more from the servants' chatter."

As the ghost faded, so, too, did Lucy's brave demeanor which she had struggled valiantly to maintain. Suspecting foul play was easier (and far more exciting) than finding out for certain that evil intentions indeed existed. But it was the prospect of losing Darrowdean, the only home Lucy had ever known and the one place which represented happy times and security, that at last overset her completely. Lucy closed her eyes and, immediately, pictures came to mind: the bright airy nursery, her little blue pony cart, the pond where she and Selinda waded in the heat of summer, the library where the sisters had so often shared their favorite books. She realized her parents were gone forever, but she had not dreamed Darrowdean would disappear as well. In the fading warmth of the October sunshine, Lucy cried as if her heart would break.


As Waverly waited for his cousin to ready himself for their outing, he wondered if he ought not to feel a little guilty for his prevarication. He had, of course, not the least intention of allowing the profligate marquess to do more than bow to Selinda before he fobbed him off on Miss Snypish. It was not, he told himself, the act of one gentleman toward another. Not that his cousin qualified for that title, naturally. Actually, he mused, it was really more an expedient measure of misleading one villain with another with the hope of serving a damsel in distress. That, surely, must settle the score. No, two wrongs don't make a right, he told himself sternly. And yet, neither would it do for Lady Selinda to languish under the repression of her gruesome family for the sake of tired convention. If things fell out awkwardly for his cousin, why, he would make it up to him. Not, he told himself as he looked ruefully about at the lavish apartment furnished almost entirely at his own expense, that Bastion didn't already owe him a staggering amount.

The Marquess of Bastion lost little time in preparing himself to accompany Lord Waverly to call at Harroweby House. As Bastion tied his cravat, he could not help but smile at the way his cousin had so stupidly fallen into serving a purpose of which he had no clue. Ah, Lady Selinda—bed her or wed her, he had told Slaverington. Either was a happy prospect, indeed. Humming to himself, he finished the knot in his cravat with a flourish and began to feel himself quite clever.

Once this toilette was completed, the cousins proceeded to their destination in Waverly's elegant barouche. They stopped briefly at the flower vendor's cart and soon presented themselves at the door of Harroweby House, nosegays in hand.

Waverly applied the door knocker and they waited. Soon, Waverly was forced to knock again. Whatever else was awry at Harroweby House, it was clear that the staff was none too efficient. He was about to knock a third time when at last the door was opened by a diminutive person with a tear-stained face.

"I am most sorry," the child apologized with an eloquent sniff, "but I am afraid I do not know where the butler has gone off to."

Not knowing quite what else to do, Lord Waverly presented Lucy with his card. "We have called to pay our respects to Lady Selinda and Miss Snypish. Are they within?"

Lucy examined the card she held carefully and looked up appraisingly at its smiling owner. "They are neither of them in just now, I'm afraid."

"Well, that settles it," said Bastion with a disappointed sigh. It seemed he had arisen from his bed for naught. Carelessly tossing his card at Lucy and a shrug at Waverly, he turned to go. "Well, I'm off, Cousin. Here, halfling, see that the ladies get their flowers. Waverly, give the brat a farthing, there's a good chap. Try again tomorrow, shall we? I'm off to my club."

With that, the marquess sauntered away, leaving Waverly and the child looking after his retreating form. "Well," Lucy pronounced at last, "there goes a villain and no mistake."

"I beg your pardon," Waverly exclaimed, stooping down to the little girl's level. "I had no idea! Are you *acquainted* with my cousin?"

"Oh, my!" Lucy cried out in sudden chagrin, covering her now crimson cheeks with her pinafore. "I beg *your* pardon, indeed. I did not mean to speak that aloud. No, I do not know the gentleman, and that was a very forward thing for me to say."

101

"It was, however, an amazingly accurate statement," he acknowledged with a slight bow. "May I present myself? I am Lord Waverly, and you, my dear, are . . . ?"

"Oh, I am just Lucy," she told him with a sad little sigh. "Lady Lucy Harroweby, I suppose, although no one here ever calls me that."

"You are Lady Selinda's sister then? I wonder . . " he mused. Then he looked closely at her. It did not take a great intellect to see that the child had been interrupted in the middle of a good cry. Waverly pulled out his pocket handkerchief and gravely handed it to her; she accepted it with an uneven grin, dabbing at the corners of her eyes and wiping her nose before handing it back.

"Won't you please come in? I do not know for certain, but Selinda may return before too long. What's more," Lucy whispered in a conspiratorial tone, "I have an idea where the sherry's kept if you should be wanting some."

"I have a better idea, Lady Lucy," Waverly preempted, suppressing a smile of amusement. "What would you say to a trip to Gunter's for some cakes and ices? Do you think it at all possible?"

Lucy thought for a moment. From what Lady Sybil had just told her it was clear that she had best be forming alliances as quickly as ever she could, regardless of the risks. It was doubtful, she reasoned, that either Aunt Prudence or Rupert would inquire after her: that was Miss Snypish's territory. Besides, she had an exceedingly good feeling about this gentleman; in fact, quite the opposite of the impression she had had of his cousin. A rare benevolence and humor radiated from him that she quite liked. By way of reply, Lucy pulled shut the door behind her and confided, "As long as we return by the back gate, I doubt any shall note my absence."

# Chapter Ten

Although Lucy was enjoying the excursion to Gunter's more than she had anything in a very long time, she was also busily directing her mental energies toward trying to read further the character of Lord Waverly. Their ride in his barouche had been beyond anything, for Lucy had not yet been able to see any of the sights of London. Although she was a garrulous child who would normally have bubbled over with conversation, she nevertheless sat prim and subdued, for she was quite aware that her presence beside him in her plain little gown and pinafore had caused a number of fashionable heads to turn. Quizzing glasses had been raised and fans tittered into, but Lord Waverly merely smiled and nodded affably to them, and continued to point out various interesting landmarks to Lucy as if there were nothing in the least untoward about her presence. This behavior alone weighed heavily in his favor.

At Gunter's, Lord Waverly had ordered ices,

lemonade, and a large tray of cakes for both of them and seemed to enjoy the repast as much as she did.

Lucy, keenly aware of Selinda's and her own predicament, decided at last that prudence had best give way to practicality and evidence to intuition. After Lucy had savored the last bit of raspberry ice, she took a deep breath and began, "I hope you will not think me too forward, Lord Waverly, but I must confide in someone and you have a face which instills confidence."

Relieved and intrigued, Waverly leaned forward and took her small hand in his, "I must say, you are no ordinary little girl, are you, Lady Lucy?"

Lucy giggled. "Not in the least. For one, I am *very* intelligent."

"That much is plain," he told her with a puzzled smile, "but it's a good deal more than that, I am sure. Well, you may tell me anything you please, Lady Lucy, and trust that I shall do my utmost to help you. Might I suggest, however, that we remove ourselves and conduct this discussion in the privacy of my barouche?"

Lucy at once recognized the wisdom of this counsel, and before long they were riding along the London streets once more.

"I could not help but notice at your sister's ball," Waverly began tentatively, "that things seemed rather oddly sorted."

"You may well say so, Lord Waverly, and what's more, I have just found out they are much worse than I ever imagined." With that, Lucy launched into a detailed description of their woes, beginning with her parents' deaths and ending with the shocking revelations to which she had been privy that morning. Quite naturally, she felt obliged to leave out all mention of Lady Sybil's spectral assistance but was a little surprised when Lord Waverly leaned over and took a close look at her ears through his quizzing glass.

"Why, how very odd! These seem to me to be quite ordinary ears," he remarked in a serious tone. "After what you have just told me, though, I had rather thought they might be shaped like keyholes!"

"Keyholes!" Lucy exclaimed indignantly. "Why, you never think I would deliberately eavesdrop do you?"

Waverly raised a skeptical eyebrow as Lucy colored, not quite knowing how to explain herself. She did not wish to tell an out-and-out plumper to her new friend and decided instead to allow a half-truth to be misinterpreted. "Well," she finally managed after some deliberation, "when a person is of my size, their presence in a room is sometimes not noted. I am sure you would be quite amazed, Lord Waverly, at the sorts of things people say right in front of children without the least notion of their hearing, much less understanding. It is little wonder we know almost as much as the servants!"

"And a very good thing that is, I must say, Lady Lucy!" Waverly declared. "Mind you, I do not disapprove of your taking advantage of whatever information comes your way. Quite the contrary, to be sure. I must apologize for teasing you just now, but you looked so sorrowful I could not bear to see it. Give me a little smile now, for your fortunes are about to change."

In her heart, Lucy felt that he was right, and, although she was not at all certain how these changes might be accomplished, Lord Waverly looked to her like a capable sort. While she was extremely gratified by Lady Sybil's efforts, she felt much better having had the opportunity to share her troubles with someone who might be able to take action outside of Harroweby House.

"As you say," Waverly went on meditatively, "there is not much time if the sale of your country estate is to be transacted so soon. Your guardians seem like a greedy pair, however, and that must mean they can be manipulated. I shall send my man of business, Mr. Noon, to Darrowdean to counter whatever offer has been made. I imagine there is an inn nearby from which he can direct our affairs?"

"The Golden Hour is generally considered best," Lucy told him. "I say, that is rare—Mr. Noon at The Golden Hour. It must be meant to be!"

"I daresay," Lord Waverly smiled at her. "He is an invaluable man, for he knows the ins and outs of all sorts of matters I have never bothered to consider. We shall see what he can do to thwart your enemies. Perhaps he could initiate a bidding war on the property. That would keep them occupied a bit longer in the country and afford us some time to maneuver. We need to gather enough evidence to present before the magistrate."

At this, Lucy heaved a huge sigh of relief, but, almost as quickly, her features darkened again as she realized that Rupert's advances had made it necessary to act even more quickly than that. Waverly looked at her sharply. "Come now, Lady Lucy. What is it you are not telling me?" he asked pointedly.

Lucy looked at him warily. It wasn't that she didn't trust his Lordship—indeed quite the opposite—but no one must ever know about the shameful episode in Rupert's chamber. She was not, of course, quite sure exactly what had transpired, but her instinct told her that whatever Rupert had attempted was beyond contempt. "It's just a feeling I have," she replied cautiously.

"Yes?" Waverly pursued.

"Well, Rupert . . ." She stopped herself abruptly. How could she begin to tell anything without telling all? "I worry that Rupert . . ."

"What about Rupert?"

"Well, Selinda is so helpless . . ."

"You worry that loathsome slug will make advances?" Waverly queried, his jaw tightening with a rage quite alien to him.

"Well," Lucy faltered helplessly, "I know he is a villain without principle and Selinda is a beauty without protection."

"No longer without protection, my dear," Waverly told her earnestly. "I shall see to that."

He had fallen in love with her, Lucy realized with sudden clarity. But so quickly she wondered? On the other hand, she reasoned loyally, how could he have helped it?

"Tell me about your sister," Waverly said quietly after a time.

"There is no one in the world like her," Lucy replied in reverent tones. "She is so beautiful and kind and amusing, but that's not all. She is so very brave, too! When Prudence and Rupert first arrived—I shall never forget it. They marched into Darrowdean with that detestable Basham on their heels. I didn't like the look of him from the very start. Indeed, I wonder how our father came to engage him. Well, you've seen Aunt Prudence and Rupert, so you know how horrible it must have been. But Selinda protected me from them, for I've such a tongue as you would not believe! But she stood between me and them, and even slapped Aunt Prudence once when she tried to cane me for calling her a fat-headed cow. Which she is!"

"Is what?"

"A fat-headed cow, of course! And for that, Selinda and I were locked in our rooms for three days with nothing but dry bread and water. I learned my lesson then. If Selinda was to suffer for my witlessness, I would have to learn to curb it. And so I have!" she concluded, her chin uplifted resolutely and her lips set.

While Lucy delivered this narrative, Lord Waverly felt himself growing more and more outraged. Hanging was too good for these rogues. It would have to be Australia! Moreover, he had thought his endeavor would merely be to find a way to court Lady Selinda and win her affection, but it was exceedingly clear now that a rescue was to be in order and quickly, too.

When Lord Waverly finally returned Lucy to her home (by the back entrance, of course), he bent for a moment over her small hand, then said, "I do not like to leave you like this, Lady Lucy. I shall try to call again tomorrow, but promise me that if anything untoward should happen or if your fears on your own or your sister's behalf should worsen, you will find some way of letting me know. I imagine we can devise some sort of signal. Let me think half a moment."

Lucy looked about her at the grounds. They were a little overgrown from their recent neglect, and the weeds poked impudently through the wrought-iron gate. "Is there a place I could hide a note back here, do you think?"

Waverly, too, began to look about. There were two stone pillars on either side of the gate upon which ivy had begun to entwine itself. "I suppose you could secrete a note within the vines here," he mused, "and I could contrive to check each day."

"I have a better plan," Lucy told him. "I'm afraid that the servants might remark the presence of a person such as yourself and tell Aunt Prudence. Our chamber window faces the front of the house. It's the last window on the third story. On the right as you face the house. If I have a message for you, I shall put some of these yellow asters in a vase and set it on the sill. That way, all you will have to do is ride by."

"A capital idea, Lucy," Waverly congratulated her. "Is there anything else I've overlooked?"

"What about rain?" she asked, her brow furrowed. "The weather has been fine of late, but I fear the damp season is not far distant."

"You're right, of course," Waverly nodded. "This is, after all, England. Perhaps I could set an oilskin pouch here later today for your use."

"Very good!" Lucy exclaimed. "You know, I begin to believe you will become an excellent intriguer before too long, sir."

"Do you think you will have any difficulty getting out of the house? You say you're watched quite closely."

Lucy thought a moment. "That *could* indeed be a problem. If it is, though, I shall just have to slip out before anyone else has arisen or after they've all gone to bed."

These arrangements made, Waverly departed, reflecting he had become a part of a most fascinating conspiracy, indeed, and had made the acquaintance of a most remarkable young lady.

All this while, Selinda's efforts had been engaged in the extremely exhausting pursuit of attempting to find a single color among the vast array offered at the modiste's that suited Miss Snypish's sallow coloring. At the same time, she endeavored to keep her wits tuned to any opportunity that might be turned to her favor on this rare outing. She had visited the shop in Bond Street on but one other occasion several years earlier, and, now, with a sinking heart, saw no one whom she recognized. Again and again her eyes looked hopefully into the face of one or another passerby, but she spotted no one even vaguely familiar. Their visit was, of course, unstylishly early in the day, but Selinda held out some small hope that someone known to her would soon enter the shop.

Her late mother's modiste, Madame Claire, had been among the most sought after in London, and Selinda had at first worried that Miss Snypish might bolt at the prospect of the extreme prices charged there. However, when she happened to glance into that lady's bulky reticule and spied a roll of bank notes the size of a three volume novel, her fears on that count were stilled, while at the same time others were engendered.

Meanwhile, Miss Motley, the anxious young assistant who had been assigned to wait on them, was despondently draping a bolt of amethyst silk about Miss Snypish's lean shoulders. The clerk pursed her lips. That shade made the poor lady's face appear quite gray. Then she tried an apple green cambric: the lady's skin merely reflected that color, making her look as if she'd just finished a nauseating Channel crossing. Valiantly, Miss Motley introduced a salmon crepe de Chine: now Miss Snypish's dismal complexion resembled a curdled sauce.

Miss Motley and Lady Selinda exchanged a fleeting glance of extreme disquiet; it seemed clear that nothing would suit, but neither wished to put a stop to the endeavor, one for the sake of her commission, the other for the continuation of her reprieve. As they fretted, Miss Snypish turned this way and that, examining her reflection with an indecipherable expression. After an agonizing period of deliberation, she delivered her astonishing resolution. "I fancy these will do very well. Now show me some trimmings, girl."

At this, Miss Motley's face lit with the brilliant expression of one who realizes she has the well-lined purse of a paperskull at her disposal; immediately she set about displaying an extensive array of Brussels laces, gilt tassels, silk flounces and fringes, as well as a wide variety of fichus, scarves, shawls, and gloves. Miss Snypish proved herself not in the least difficult to please, as it turned out, although Miss Motley soon learned that the less appealing her patron was likely to appear in an item, the more likely was she to purchase it.

Although Selinda had found it essential to her peace of mind over the past six months to banish as nearly as humanly possible all the thoughts of injustice and vengeance that arose from her situation, a searing wrath arose in her breast as she now watched Miss Snypish posing in a mirror under the brim of a sweet gypsy bonnet trimmed in ribbons of a delicate willow green. Selinda could only conjecture how she herself would look in such a confection. She appeased her jealousy to some small extent, however, by reflecting with uncharacteristic rancor that her horrid companion resembled more closely a sly rat peering out from under a leaf of lettuce than a fetching bohemian. Still, the sight rankled.

When Miss Snypish had finally ceased her preening, she handed the assistant a wad of bank notes, adjuring her to have the dresses made up as quickly as possible.

"And to which address shall I direct their delivery?" Miss Motley asked.

Miss Snypish paused a moment in thought. It would not do for anyone at Harroweby House to note either her purchases or speculate about her ability to afford them. "I believe I shall come and collect them myself," she said briefly. "Good day to you. Come along, Lady Selinda."

Once out on the street again, the companion turned to Selinda and, in tones tinged with religious ardor, said, "I had no idea such places existed. I vow I shall never wear gray again."

Seizing on this relatively companionable moment, Selinda remarked, "I am glad to have been able to assist you. It is such a fine day, is it not, Miss Snypish. How long do you suppose we have until we must return?"

Suddenly suspicious, Miss Snypish turned on her. "Why do you wish to know?"

Selinda had indeed been wishing to prolong their outing even though the hope of recognizing someone who had known her parents had waned. She had known all along that this was a slim possibility, indeed, for she had met very few of their acquaintances, but it was the very sort of thing that reading romantic novels had encouraged her to look for. Surely the fates could not be so cruel as to bestow on her a life entirely devoid of coincidence! "Why, Miss Snypish," she replied in injured tones, "I thought you might wish to step down the street to Cosgrove's. My mother always spoke highly of their fine soaps."

Satisfied for the moment that her charge was not plotting anything untoward, Miss Snypish nodded her head. "I doubt I shall be wanted for another hour or so," she reflected. "Come, show me the way."

Before too long, Miss Snypish proved herself to be as susceptible to the allure of Mr. Cosgrove's fine soaps and fragrances as she had been to the wares offered by Miss Motley. Not only did she avail herself of several boxes of scented savonettes but also chose an assortment of perfumed waters, oils, sachets, rouges, powders, and a potent plaster said to be efficacious in the removal of unwanted hair. As Selinda stood back and watched the assembly of this awe-inspiring arsenal, she wondered distractedly whether and to what extent she might be called upon to play Pygmalion to this unlikely Galatea.

# Chapter Eleven

Lady Sybil had been beside herself with excitement and nervous curiosity ever since the moment she spied Lucy drive off so mysteriously with Lord Waverly. Whatever could it mean, she wondered? With a flutter of anticipation, she had, of course, recognized the handsome gentleman from Selinda's ball. Used as she was to an existence devoted to diversion, the ghost had found recent events somewhat dampening, despite her keen interest. Thus she was now in high alt that, at last, something pleasant and perhaps even promising seemed to be in the offing.

After the marked success of her morning's eavesdropping—however unnerving its revelations had been—the ghost had been disappointed to find that nothing of any note had been discussed in the servants' domain. They seemed to be, for the most part, an exceedingly lazy, churlish bunch, more concerned with avoiding work and lining their own pockets than attending to their duties.

These they performed with such amazing inattention that the likelihood of their garnering gossip of even the most superficial variety was highly unlikely. Moreover, from what she had thus far seen of the household's operations, Lady Sybil doubted that any of the ill-sorted crew had had the least exposure to the workings of a well-run establishment. So, she decided open-mindedly, it was really not their fault if they were ignorant of the time-honored custom of servants' hall rumor-mongering.

All the while she waited for Lucy to return from her mysterious outing, the ghost had paced nervously about the gallery, their prearranged rendezvous. How in heaven's name, Lady Sybil wondered, had she ever managed to fill her time before the arrival of her newly found descendants? Her activities and observations during the previous hundred years or so had never seemed so very tedious, but, in comparison to the events of the week just past, they really must have been, she decided.

The intensity of the current Harroweby troubles notwithstanding, the girls really were a most endearing and engaging pair. It was more than that, though. Lady Sybil now realized that she already felt an overwhelming affection for them, as well as an uncharacteristic sense of duty. Prior to their arrival, her ghostly machinations had been altogether self-serving—performed solely for the purpose of whatever diversion they might afford her. What flirtations and liaisons were in the offing and how might she promote them? There was, of course, that same element here, but so much more was at stake! Indeed, she felt her present efforts to be quite valiant. Now, as she waited impatiently for Lucy's return, time (and her newly cultivated sense of matriarchal distress) hung heavily indeed on her unworldly hands. By the time the child's footsteps at last echoed along the musty hallway, it seemed as if several more centuries must have passed.

"You will not credit it, Lady Sybil," Lucy bubbled as she skipped in, her little face alight with excitement. "What a wondrous day it has been! I have just been out riding and dining with a veritable paragon!"

"Oh, yes, I am well aware of Lord Waverly's charms," the ghost assured her, breathless with relief and anticipation, "and I agree most heartily. In fact, were I but a hundred years younger . . ."

"Or I a few years older . . ." Lucy mused with a mischievous grin.

". . . our poor Selinda would do well to have a care for her interests," Lady Sybil finished with a flourish of her fan.

"Well, I doubt we should have very much success in that quarter," Lucy confided, "for it is the most amazing thing ever: Lord Waverly is top over tails in love with Selinda!"

"What! Surely he did not tell you so?"

"He did not have to. It came to me in a blinding flash as he was speaking of her. I know that flash of old and I know I am not mistaken."

"I hope not indeed," the ghost declared, her voice edged with doubt, "for I believe he is the very

118

gentleman for her. I thought as much when I watched them dance together the other night. I wish you might have seen them. They moved as one!"

"Well, you needn't worry, Lady Sybil. I know I am not wrong, at least, in this case," Lucy said earnestly. Then she sighed and a slight frown of worry appeared. "All we need to ascertain is the state of Selinda's affections. I wonder how her heart stands. Do you believe her affections can possibly have been engaged as well?"

"If they have not been," the ghost pronounced with confidence, "I shall make certain that they soon enough are."

Lucy climbed up into a dusty window seat and crossed her legs. "How do you propose to accomplish that?"

"Ah, you forget, my dear," Lady Sybil smiled. "Dreams are my special talent."

"A romantic dream!" Lucy exclaimed. "The very thing indeed! I know it may be ill luck, but I almost begin to believe we shall prevail in all things at last. Now then, I have told Lord Waverly *almost* everything about our trials. I think it best he does not know about *you*, of course! The effect of our conversation is this: he has promised to help Selinda and me with Darrowdean and anything else he can manage. We have even contrived a way to exchange messages. Oh, you cannot imagine, Lady Sybil! He is so pleasant and kind. He *even* called me Lady Lucy with the utmost civility and drove me about the city, even though we drew all sorts of impertinent stares. I believe he is almost worthy of Selinda."

"If any man is *ever* worthy of a woman, it may be he," the ghost agreed.

"Everything seems to be falling into place then. Did you find out anything belowstairs?"

"Very little, unfortunately. Only that your wretched guardians are being robbed and ill-served as scandalously as they deserve."

"Hmm," Lucy frowned. "I suppose that only means Selinda's and my interests are being attacked on yet one more front, for you must remember it is our fortune being abused here. Gracious, sometimes it seems there's not a soul about who doesn't have a hand in it. Is there no end to wickedness?"

"Not in my experience," Lady Sybil sighed philosophically. "The only thing to do, I suppose, is to turn one evil against the other. We already know that there is contention and counterplotting among the conspirators. They do not trust each other you know—a few well-designed dreams, and we can perhaps turn their suspicions to our own purposes. By the bye, one thing we shall need to do is find a means for you to carry one of my former possessions about with you. I should like to follow you out if the opportunity presents itself again. I suppose we cannot have you toting a piece of furniture about. I wonder . . . where can all my jewelry have gone?"

Rupert's mother had in the meantime sat for several hours playing set after set of patience, the corners of her mouth anchored down at an alarming angle. In the past, the game's monotonous pattern had often helped soothe her nerves and focus her attention. She had "learned patience in prison," she was fond of saying to herself with a bitter laugh. In that dismal keep, the game had helped her while away many a tedious hour. At her elbow now sat a half-empty glass of gin. That expedient had always provided a sure, if transitory, source of additional solace.

The red saloon's heavy curtains were still drawn against the brightness of the blue autumn day: sunlight had always depressed Prudence. Moreover, this morning's interview with her wayward son, Rupert, had distressed her at her heart's core.

Prudence had begun the day in a foul temper and her seething displeasure was growing by the minute. She had been cursing her short-sightedness for some days now. Lapses of good sense were unusual for her and, since the outset of this adventure, the most promising of her life, she had made a number of ill-judged decisions. She now realized that it had been altogether unnecessary to bring the two girls along with them to the city. She would have done much better to have left them sequestered somewhere in the country, but at the time, there had seemed to be many important reasons to keep them with her.

Of all the Harroweby properties, Darrowdean was the least prominent and least likely to attract the interest of interfering do-gooders. It was a secluded property, and the only neighbors seemed to be a doddering squire and his wife who rarely ventured out. Had the sale of the estate not been so tempting, it would have been an admirable place from which to execute her plans. The lands were rich, though, the manor attractive, and, best of all, it was not part of any entail. The prospect of easily gotten wealth had been too tempting for Prudence's avaricious soul. She had considered, of course, placing the girls at one of the other estates, but she was unsure how much interest their sudden arrival might arouse. She knew she would have to take Selinda to London for her Season eventually, for she was at first quite careful to play the role of an interested, albeit heavy-handed, relation, respecting in most ways the dictates of the Harroweby will. She might just as well, she had decided, use their absence from the country to her advantage.

What a fool she'd been! A Season in London indeed! That, her hindsight now told her, could quite simply have been got around. The Harroweby sisters were more easily bullied than she had at first thought six months ago. Threaten harm to either and the other would comply with anything. No, the presence of the girls in the city, particularly Selinda's, had caused Prudence nothing but trouble. Despite her words of reassurance to Rupert, she was afraid that someone might have become interested in Selinda's situation. She could ill afford meddling if she and Rupert were to make their escape with what fortune they had amassed intact.

And Rupert! Rupert! He had disappointed her very badly indeed this morning. Well, she had spoiled the lad villainously, but in exchange she had always expected unfaltering loyalty. Drat that wretched Harroweby girl with all her mincing ways! What rankled most, after all, was that Prudence knew she had been wrong once more. Forcing a marriage between Selinda and Rupert had been her idea to begin with. It had certainly seemed the least complicated means of acquiring a fortune. Even so, Rupert had at first been reluctant to leg-shackle himself; that is, until he had actually clapped eyes on the little minx. Then it was a different story altogether.

Since their first meeting, it seemed he could think of nothing else but possessing the chit. At first, Prudence had dangled the girl in front of him like a choice bonbon. He had been quick indeed to lick his lips in anticipation. Only lately, however, had she begun to regret her scheme. Rupert was now not only bewitched, but out and out rebellious as well.

For twenty-five years, Rupert had been her sole consolation, her pride, her companion, and her joy. She had sacrificed everything for his well-being and happiness; petted and praised him, as well. He had been born mere days after her release from prison, a tangible souvenir of her futile attempt to bribe a guard with her body. Afterwards, she had for a time tread the boards at a number of run-down theaters, having discovered a talent for acting and dialects that had served her very well over the years. Later, when her figure had run to fat, she'd turned her agile hand to stealing what she could. It had been a hard life, she reflected bitterly, but the end of her troubles was in sight.

She was not about to lose either her chance to enjoy a fortune or her son's affections because of some slip of a spoiled heiress.

Oh, she knew how it would be. Once the pair married, she would be consigned to the background at best, no longer heeded, no longer the most important force in Rupert's life. Well, she frowned unpleasantly, she would as soon see him hang as see him doting on that privileged little seductress.

Prudence continued to turn the cards relentlessly, her bitterness eating away at her spirits, until a slight rap came at the door. "Enter," she commanded morosely as she brushed aside an acidic tear of self-pity. "Oh, it's only you, Snypish. Well, what is it?"

"You asked to see me when I returned," the companion stated with prim civility beneath which resided a vigorous sense of loathing. She would be very glad to rid herself at last of this repellent role of subservience. Before long, she told herself with an inner smile, the fortune she had quietly been accumulating and the connection she hoped to make with Lord Waverly's cousin, the Marquess of Bastion, would make her the beneficiary of the same kind of groveling and fawning she had been forced to perform herself. The prospect made her heart race with excitement. She had landed on her feet this time and no mistake.

"Oh. Yes," the other replied flatly, barely acknowledging her. "We have some arrangements to make. My son and I shall be departing the day after tomorrow. We shall be absent for some two or three days at the most. During that time, no one—

no one at all, mind you—is to stir from this house. There are, of course, to be no visitors."

Well, we shall see about that, Miss Snypish thought rebelliously to herself. The combined effects of her shopping expedition and being greeted upon her return by gentlemen's cards and flowers (both of which she had seized upon without the least thought of Selinda's interest) had fed the fantasies she had lately been nursing and set her on a path from which there was no return. She would go wherever she pleased and see whomever should happen to call, and hell take any who tried to stop her. In spite of these inner ragings, she nevertheless held her peace and silently nodded her habitual compliance. "Where will you be going, madam?" she asked, taking considerable pains to keep her voice carefully neutral.

"That is none of your concern, Snypish, is it?" the other woman snapped. "If for any reason you should need to communicate with me, you need only send a note round to Mr. Basham's offices."

Miss Snypish thought quickly. Her employers' absence, albeit a brief one, would offer her the opportunity not only to receive visitors in privacy, but would also provide the time she needed to complete several important business arrangements that had been pending until such a moment. She would just as soon eliminate as many of her duties as possible. "Might I suggest, madam, that, wherever you are going, you take Lady Lucy along with you?"

"Lucy? That annoying baggage!" Prudence snorted dismissively. "Whatever for?"

"You do not wish visitors, nor will you allow any of us to leave the premises. I am not negligent in my duties by any means, but even I cannot watch both of them twenty-four hours a day. Moreover," she went on in a significant tone, "I have of late interrupted more than one whispered conference between the pair. Indeed, I believe them to be plotting some sort of mischief. Trust me, those two are up to anything! If you wish to guarantee Lady Selinda's continued docility and obedience during your absence, I would suggest you take her sister with you."

Prudence thought for a moment, then nodded. It would be useful to have a ready threat to ensure Selinda's compliance. She could not afford any trouble now. Moreover, having the child alone with her in the country would provide the opportunity to even the old score between them. More than once she'd intercepted Lucy's rebellious glances, and the child had never made secret her opinion of her supposed aunt. In the seclusion of Darrowdean, these offenses could be answered. A good whipping and a bread and water confinement would be the very thing for the little brat. Prudence's countenance cleared considerably as she envisioned Lucy's future sufferings. Life did offer some moments of satisfaction.

"I believe you may have something there, Snypish. Very well, then. I shall take the child, but have a care and do not mention this decision to anyone. I haven't the patience to listen to tirades.

Be prepared to pack a valise for the child when I give the word. She needn't know a thing until just before she's led to the carriage."

Rupert, for his part, had also spent the remainder of the day brooding. His mother, he grumbled inwardly, bore watching. He didn't at all fancy her beastly meddling in his affairs and he would be damned if he would allow her to interfere with his plans for Selinda or her fortune. Absconding with a few thousand pounds and pulling a leg for some godforsaken colony or other was not at all what he had in mind. Besides, he intended more for Selinda than the mere deflowering his mother had alluded to. A marriage to her could answer all of his appetites: lust, lucre, and lofty ambition.

The first of these went without saying. Selinda was certainly a choice little morsel and the very memory of her trim body writhing in his arms yesterday still generated a film of fevered perspiration on his upper lip and a severe tightening about the loins. He had been so close, dammit! He shut his eyes and heaved a ragged sigh. His time would come before too long. Yes, he could well imagine *years* of satisfaction from that quarter.

Second, while he was quite certain his mother had been characteristically acquisitive in the short time she'd had access to the estate coffers, whatever she had managed to accumulate—even with the complicity of Basham—could not possibly rival the potential available. True, the sale of Dar-rowdean would very likely fetch a pretty penny, but there were other estates and properties, and perhaps even vaults filled with plate as well. Who, after all, knew what Basham was keeping for himself? Piles and piles of riches, very likely. Then why, Rupert asked himself reasonably, settle for thousands of pounds when one might have tens of thousands?

Last, though, it came to ambition. With Selinda as his wife, Rupert could enter those circles heretofore closed to him. He could affect—nay, actually live—the life of a gentleman, just as he had always dreamed. From earliest childhood, Rupert had felt himself destined for great things, but for years he had been weighed down by his mother's shameful past and tawdry connections. It was high time he cut loose from the old harridan. Delving into a box of honeyed comfits, he wondered idly if there were an oubliette at Darrowdean.

*Rosamonde's eyes glowed in the moonlight,* Waverly was reading, *and her alabaster brow shone like marble. Looking deeply into Roderick's eyes, she read there the love she had ever sought but which had heretofore eluded her. Her mind cast back over the time since he had entered her life, first as the distant, aloof Duke of Duncarlyle, then as the mysterious masked Roderico, fiery and passionate. In the first guise, he had perceived the misery of her untenable circumstances as the victim of her guardian's scalding obsession. Then, he had undertaken to deliver her from Black-*

# MORE PASSION AND ADVENTURE AWAIT... YOUR TRIP TO A BIG ADVENTUROUS WORLD BEGINS WHEN YOU ACCEPT YOUR FIRST 4 NOVELS ABSOLUTELY *FREE*
## (AN $18.00 VALUE)

Accept your Free gift and start to experience more of the passion and adventure you like in a historical romance novel. Each Zebra novel is filled with proud men, spirited women and tempestuous love that you'll remember long after you turn the last page.

Zebra Historical Romances are the finest novels of their kind. They are written by authors who really know how to weave tales of romance and adventure in the historical settings you love. You'll feel like you've actually gone back in time with the thrilling stories that each Zebra novel offers.

## GET YOUR FREE GIFT WITH THE START OF YOUR HOME SUBSCRIPTION

Our readers tell us that these books sell out very fast in book stores and often they miss the newest titles. So Zebra has made arrangements for you to receive the four newest novels published each month.

You'll be guaranteed that you'll never miss a title, and home delivery is so convenient. And to show you just how easy it is to get Zebra Historical Romances, we'll send you your first 4 books absolutely FREE! Our gift to you just for trying our home subscription service.

## BIG SAVINGS AND FREE HOME DELIVERY

Each month, you'll receive the four newest titles as soon as they are published. You'll probably receive them even before the bookstores do. What's more, you may preview these exciting novels free for 10 days. If you like them as much as we think you will, just pay the low preferred subscriber's price of just $3.75 each. *You'll save $3.00 each month off the publisher's price.* AND, your savings are even greater because there are never any shipping, handling or other hidden charges—FREE Home Delivery. Of course you can return any shipment within 10 days for full credit, no questions asked. There is no minimum number of books you must buy.

# 4 FREE BOOKS

## TO GET YOUR 4 FREE BOOKS WORTH $18.00 — MAIL IN THE FREE BOOK CERTIFICATE T O D A Y

Fill in the Free Book Certificate below, and we'll send your FREE BOOKS to you as soon as we receive it.

If the certificate is missing below, write to: Zebra Home Subscription Service, Inc., P.O. Box 5214, 120 Brighton Road, Clifton, New Jersey 07015-5214.

---

## FREE BOOK CERTIFICATE
## 4 FREE BOOKS
### ZEBRA HOME SUBSCRIPTION SERVICE, INC.

**YES!** Please start my subscription to Zebra Historical Romances and send me my first 4 books absolutely FREE. I understand that each month I may preview four new Zebra Historical Romances free for 10 days. If I'm not satisfied with them, I may return the four books within 10 days and owe nothing. Otherwise, I will pay the low preferred subscriber's price of just $3.75 each; a total of $15.00, *a savings off the publisher's price of $3.00.* I may return any shipment and I may cancel this subscription at any time. There is no obligation to buy any shipment and there are no shipping, handling or other hidden charges. Regardless of what I decide, the four free books are mine to keep.

NAME

ADDRESS _____ APT _____

CITY _____ STATE _____ ZIP _____

( )
TELEPHONE _____

SIGNATURE _____ (if under 18, parent or guardian must sign)

ZB0593

Terms, offer and prices subject to change without notice. Subscription subject to acceptance by Zebra Books. Zebra Books reserves the right to reject any order or cancel any subscription.

*thorne's advances, only to succumb to the silent passions concealed beneath their otherwise tranquil demeanors. Rosamonde felt herself drawn toward him, into his arms, beyond all control, all hope . . .*

Waverly wiped his brow and exhaled unevenly. Little wonder, he reflected, that Lady Selinda had had such difficulty devoting her attention to church services. This was heady stuff and, he was quite sure, altogether improper. How nice for a change! Lord Waverly read on with marked attention.

Unaware that his imagination followed the same path as Selinda's as he read, he, too, envisioned himself in the role of Roderick, paying court to a Rosamonde who was very much the image of Selinda. As page gave way to page, he filled in such little details as the author of that text had referred to but euphemistically. By the last chapter, Lord Waverly had an exceedingly precise picture in mind of what loving Selinda might be like.

As he closed the book, Waverly turned his mind to Selinda's situation. Much of it seemed to be mirrored in the plot in which he had just been immersed. Was that, he wondered, another reason the story had held her so rapt? In the book, Rosamonde had been set upon by unscrupulous villains and rescued by an intrepid duke. True, there were villains aplenty in today's world, villains worthy of any sensational novel. But heroes? Were there any more heroes?

A hundred schemes for Selinda's deliverance

whirled about in his head, but each seemed more mundane than the next. Of course, he would send his man of business to Darrowdean as he had promised, and he would do his best to see that Selinda and Lucy's guardians were brought to justice, but he feared it would take more than that to truly win Selinda's heart. He'd seen enough of desperation to know that she might be persuaded to marry him out of a survival instinct or, worse yet, out of gratitude. That would never do. He would have to think about this. Perhaps Lucy would have some ideas.

Lucy certainly had. Before she was sent up to bed that evening, she had managed to return to the back entrance where she discovered the oilskin pouch secreted among the vines just as Lord Waverly had promised. Inside she found five shiny gold sovereigns and a note. It read:

> *My dear Lady Lucy,*
> *I hope that the enclosed coins may be of some use to you—it never hurts to have a little of the ready at one's disposal. I shall keep good watch at your window for any sign of yellow asters.*
>
> > *God bless you,*
> > *Waverly*

Lucy smiled to herself as she realized how comforting the weight of the gold coins felt in her little hand. She must take care to see that her wealth was not discovered. It might be very helpful if she should have to bribe a servant or hire a hackney. She had not yet determined whether it was wise to tell Selinda about her acquaintance with Lord Waverly. She did not think her sister would disapprove, of course, but she knew that Selinda worried inordinately about her and tried whenever possible to shoulder all the burdens of their difficult situation herself. Perhaps it would be best to wait and see.

Before she turned to go in again, Lucy took the precaution of picking a small bouquet of the flowers which were to be her distress signal, if needed. It couldn't hurt to be prepared since she could hardly imagine having such an opportunity should a real crisis arise.

As she made her way up the stairs to bed a few moments later, she remembered that tonight Lady Sybil would try her hand at altering dreams. Selinda's, she knew, was bound to be delightful, and, come to think of it, she wouldn't mind a nice one herself. She sincerely hoped, however, whatever the ghost had in mind for Rupert and his mother would set them on their tails!

# *Chapter Twelve*

Selinda did not quite know how she had found herself in the meadow, hazy with a blue froth of forget-me-nots, but as she lay in the deep green grass and gazed up into the depths of the sky, she felt as if she had never truly been at peace before. A few white clouds drifted by, and she smiled as she watched them. The sun shone down, warm, brilliant, and reassuring. She almost felt as if she were floating.

As she lay there, she found she was dressed in a light and airy gown, so light indeed that it seemed as if it might blow away as easily as a wisp of down. Amazingly, as soon as that thought had formed, a playful breeze came up and her gown floated away with it. She suddenly found herself dressed only in her chemise and a pair of little kid gloves. That was a comfort anyway, she thought. Despite her surprise at her sudden state of dishabillé, Selinda found herself unexpectedly composed. Then, turning lazily onto her side and raising up on one elbow, she found herself face-to-face with Lord Waverly in much the same manner as she had done under the pew in church. How singular!

He was fully clothed, she noted abstractedly, and she wondered if he didn't find her state of near undress just the least bit odd. He smiled at her slowly and reassuringly, though, as he gathered her into his arms and kissed her very gently in the warm sunlight. How lovely it felt to be held! On one distant level, she realized this odd circumstance had to be very, very wrong, but, oh, it did feel so very, very right.

The kiss seemed to go on forever before it gradually became deeper, and, to her dismay, she felt her lips very gently part beneath his. She had never thought of such a penetrating kiss, but this, too, felt quite natural and enjoyable. Slowly she gave herself up to the embrace; bit by bit, she allowed herself to respond to his hands which were delicately tracing the lines of her back and thighs. In spite of the sun's warmth, she shivered and gasped as Waverly cupped one of her breasts and caressed it luxuriously for several long moments. What an extraordinary to-do! Selinda had never imagined that such a thing might happen, but it felt exquisite. All the while, he continued to kiss her in a decidedly thorough manner. Slowly she felt herself arch and moan.

"Selinda!" a voice whispered. "Selinda!"

She felt herself being shaken urgently. Selinda opened her eyes to the blackness of her chamber.

"Wake up, Selinda! You must have been having

the most terrible nightmare," Lucy told her in some confusion. What on earth was Lady Sybil about? She had thought this was to be a nice dream. "Why, you've been thrashing about and moaning like anything. And it took me forever to wake you!"

Selinda groaned. In the darkness, Lady Sybil joined her. What a lovely dream she'd created. And, oh! what a plaguey thing it was that Lucy had interrupted it. She certainly had not anticipated that sort of development. Well, she had done her very best. She knew it was certainly a dream to carry *her* heart away, but would it do for Selinda? A tiny shiver of doubt crept over her. The ghost was vaguely aware that Selinda was somewhat less worldly than she had been at a similar age. For that reason, she had taken some pains to rein in her very sensual imagination. After all, she reminded herself virtuously, she had made sure that the gentleman in the dream had kept his breeches on. The memory of her own maidenhood was quite blurry, though; what, she wondered, had chasteness been like? It had been so fleeting. Well, the dream was done now, so it didn't truly signify, did it? She only hoped that her efforts had been sufficient to promote a *tendre*.

In the darkness, Lucy had turned over and gone back to sleep, but Selinda now sat upright in bed, cradling her face in her hands. She was anything but ready to return to her slumbers. Dear Heavens! She was worse than any strumpet not only to have somehow summoned up such a shocking dream in her imagination, but to have enjoyed it, too! She

134

must indeed be a very, very bad sort of girl. The very worst sort! Shameless! She could almost weep but restrained herself for fear of Lucy awakening once again. Ever since Rupert's scandalous attempt on her virtue, she told herself, she had tumbled into the depths of depravity. First, there were her designs on poor, innocent Lord Waverly, and now this disgraceful dream. Was there any hope for her? And yet . . . it seemed Lord Waverly might well be her only hope. She really did not wish to ensnare the gentleman, but it seemed too much to ask that he might simply fall in love as inexorably as she seemed to be doing. Oh! It was all too perplexing!

In the opposite wing of Harroweby House, Lady Sybil now turned her efforts to the more sinister members of the household. As far as she was concerned, Rupert's lascivious scheming presented the most imminent threat to Selinda's well-being. Therefore, she must not only heighten his distrust of his compatriots, but also somehow steer him away from the girl. She feared that might be a more complicated task than she was equal to. Perhaps it would be best to enter his dream and see what sort of material there was to work with, she decided, as she followed the discordant sound of wheezing snores into his chamber.

Lady Sybil stood for a moment over his bulky form and concentrated. Well, she thought to herself as his dream took shape before her, it might well have been worse. Over the years, she had found it altogether remarkable how many men of a lecherous bent dreamed about eating.

In his dream, Rupert sat at the head of a long table, surrounded by great trays laden with roasts and puddings overflowing with gravies and sauces, and was busily stuffing his mouth with both hands. As he did so, the sounds of his piggish grunting filled the air. Inspired, Lady Sybil wrinkled her delicate nose with disdain and went to work at once.

I must eat it all, Rupert was telling himself desperately, every scrap, or I shall get no dessert! Out in the kitchen, he knew there was a blanc-mange as big as a house, all moist and quivery, just the way he liked it. What a rotten thing it was that his mother wouldn't let him start with sweets. As he finished off one tray of food, he pounded his fists on the table for the next before he had even finished swallowing.

Before too long, he found that it was getting quite difficult to hold onto his utensils, for his hands were beginning to alter second by second: indeed, they were beginning to look quite like cloven hooves. That doesn't signify, Rupert snorted to himself, I can eat faster without 'em. Straightaway, he plunged headlong into the steaming plate before him, biting into the meat and rooting up the vegetables with the very handy tusks he seemed to have suddenly sprouted.

Lady Sybil grimaced as she observed bits of meat and other victuals flying about. As were all the dreams she tampered with, this one had become extremely vivid—it was all she could do to keep from ducking the imaginary scraps. All the while, of course, Rupert's transformation was progressing with alarming speed. By this time, his nose had become a long snout, his ears drooped, and a pert pink tail curled at his posterior. Well, she thought to herself, I believe this piggy has foraged long enough.

"Sausages!" A familiar cry rang through the dining hall, followed by the sound of relentless footsteps. "Sausages on the hoof! After him, fools!"

Rupert rose up from his platter with an alarmed snort. His mother, scowling even more barbarously than was her wont, appeared to be coming for him with a pack of fierce dogs. She was flanked by Miss Snypish toting a blunderbuss and Mr. Basham with a large net. As quickly as he could, the ungainly swine started from his chair, upsetting the table and sending plates flying as his hooves scraped and skidded along the slippery floor. He raced as fast as his stout little legs would carry him up the stairs and down the everlengthening corridor to his chamber. When at last he reached it, however, the door burst open: somehow the fiends had arrived before him!

He turned abruptly, raced down the stairs, and made for the sculpture garden. There, his heart beating wildly, he stood with wobbly effort on his hind legs, hoping to blend in among the statuaries. It was to no avail, however, for the marble figures, too, turned on him, coming to life with ravenous expressions on their carved faces. One by one, they stepped down from their pedestals and came for him. He turned again and sped toward the maze. Perhaps he could lose them there. Right, right, left, right again. Before long, he was in the center, but he could hear the voices of his pursuers not far away and gaining on him rapidly. Where could he go? Where could he hide? Looking about him again, he noticed Selinda was now seated primly on a little bench, daintily eating a plate of blancmange.

"Would you like a bite, little piggy?" she asked sweetly, extending a forkful.

Hide me! he tried to tell her, but all that emerged was a high-pitched squeal. The pack was almost upon him. He squealed again, louder and louder.

"Good for you, Selinda," his mother pronounced as she rounded the corner of the hedge and marched into the center of the maze. "You've got him for us. He will feed us all winter."

Rupert froze in his tracks, unable to move for some unaccountable reason as his mother's pack surrounded him, showing their wet, sharp teeth.

"Poor little piggy!" Selinda smiled at him, tears brimming in her eyes. "I could almost find it in my heart to help you if you did not look so much like my cousin Rupert. He did me such an ill turn as you cannot guess. Why, do you know, I was half in love with him until he tried to take advantage of me! Now it will take a good deal for him to find himself in my good graces again, and only I can save him." She sighed, slipped a silk lead about his neck, and handed him over to his mother, who raised a shining knife above his head.

Rupert reared up in bed, sweating feverishly, his heart pounding. He had never dreamed anything like that before. It was so horrible and so real! Gingerly he touched his face and ears to reassure himself. What on earth could it mean? He was sure there was some unusual significance to it, for he was never one to disregard signs and portents. Great men dreamed such foreboding dreams as this. He would certainly have to find his way over to Whitechapel in the morning to have his cards read.

He felt shakingly sick with fear as he leaned back against his pillows and forced himself to review the dream's content. What if Selinda's good graces were instrumental to his future? Perhaps he had acted too hastily yesterday. Almost in love with him? That he could well believe, for he thought himself quite a fine fellow. Perhaps she had only been trying to make him jealous at the ball. Of course! That only made good sense! Well, he would certainly have to apologize to her and begin to court her prettily, regardless of what his mama thought. That ogress was not to be trusted anyway. The dream had made that much clear.

Lady Sybil, quite content with her handiwork in Rupert's slumbers, now drifted along to his mother's chamber. She shuddered to think what that noxious person's dreams might reveal. To her dismay, however, she found Prudence still wide awake and busily occupied in sewing thick stacks of bank notes into the voluminous skirts of a traveling dress. There must be a small fortune in the dress already from the looks of it.

Frowning, the ghost was about to make her exit

when her eye was caught by a gleaming little pile on the bed. Jewels! Rubies, amethysts, and pearls gleamed in the dim light. Some pieces she did not recognize, but there were enough of her own glimmering among them to make it evident that this horrid woman had her fingers in more pots than one. Making off with money was one thing, but the family jewels! This was a sad crime indeed. Looking more closely at the silent seamstress, Lady Sybil was incensed to perceive her own lovely pearl pomander hanging among the fleshy folds of the woman's neck. This desecration was beyond enough! Oh! she would not be satisfied until that one was well behind bars, and her gluttonish son along with her.

Prudence stopped for a moment in her endeavor and shivered. It was odd, she thought, that the room had suddenly become so icy. There must be a draft coming down the chimney. Before long, she reflected with a complacent shrug, she'd be in the tropics and would never suffer from the dank British climate again. She'd build a palace—you could stretch the blunt like catgut in the tropics, she'd heard—and have a hundred slaves to do her bidding as well. The sun would put some color into her cheeks and perhaps some impoverished noble or other would beg for her hand. Not that she wanted or needed any man, of course. But the thought of some lord or other squirming under her repressive thumb mightily took her fancy. She could hardly wait for the pleasures ahead.

# Chapter Thirteen

The fine weather the residents of Harroweby House had been enjoying for the past month gave way the next morning to the perennial gray and damp which would, in all likelihood, hold sway until the spring. Waking to rain-washed windows, each one did his or her best to conceal the nervous energy engendered by the air of change; nevertheless, the sound of rainfall in the courtyard echoed in their pulses.

The morning passed with relative placidity, all things considered, each member of the household going about his or her own business with varying degrees of feigned serenity. Beneath their placid demeanors, there was not, of course, a single heart unseared by some emotion or another, whether it was fear, excitement, or chagrin.

After an exceedingly wretched night, Rupert finally abandoned hopes of sleeping in and began the day intent on modifying his manners toward Selinda. The haunting shadow of the previous

141

night's dream had risen up before him as soon as he opened his eyes that morning. It was not a pretty prospect. He was just as certain in broad daylight as he had been during the night that the dream had been a warning of his mother's murderous intentions as well as a sign that pointed the only way to his deliverance. In addition to keeping an even keener eye on his perfidious parent, therefore, he was now determined to adopt a chivalrous air and placatory manner in all of his dealings with his lovely cousin.

Making his way downstairs, he was unnerved to find that his mother had preceded him at the breakfast table. Neither of them was an early riser, or course, and they sized each other up rather suspiciously as they exchanged cursory good mornings.

"There are sausages on the sideboard," his mother told him.

Rupert's stomach did a lurching flip-flop as he quickly dropped the lid of the chafing dish. Instead he poured a cup of stout tea and sat down for the first time in his life determined not to break his fast. The very thought of food was altogether too gruesome, really.

They sat in silence for some minutes, each surreptitiously stealing glances at the other, until at last Selinda made her entrance. She stopped short in the doorway, surprised to see the pair at this early hour. If she'd had the least clue they would be about she'd have kept to her chamber and shared a bit of Lucy's breakfast, meager though that portion was.

As soon as he spied her, Rupert rose abruptly to his feet and bowed as deeply as his girth allowed, then pulled a chair back for her. Selinda proceeded with caution, gingerly settling herself while Rupert busily poured her tea and offered to fill her plate for her. She accepted a scone and a little fruit, eschewing the despised sausages, much to Rupert's intense gratification. This, too, he felt sure was significant.

"Did you sleep well, little cousin?" he asked with what he supposed to be a winsome smile.

Selinda suppressed a shudder: the memory of *her* dream in conjunction with those conjured up by the sight of her odious cousin put her quite ill at ease.

Rupert bit his lower lip. Considering his recent treatment of her, it was little wonder the girl shuddered. Drat his mother for driving him to such desperate measures. It was all her fault. Now, he must do something to win back Selinda's affections and trust, for he believed implicitly in the dream's revelation that both had once been his. If he could not, he feared that his ambitions would suddenly be beyond his grasp, just when they seemed so close. He knit his eyebrows violently as he tried to think. He must find some way to talk to Selinda privately and apologize for his actions. Then he must ply her with presents and flowers. Pretty compliments and comfits. Outings and such. That would surely do the trick.

"I shall be driving out today, Cousin. Do you think you would care to accompany me?"

Selinda swallowed hard. The last thing she wanted was a private meeting with her cousin. She entertained very little hope that she would emerge from such an encounter unscathed. "I find myself a little unwell this morning, Cousin. I hope you will forgive me, but perhaps another time would be better."

"Ah, but I shall be driving in Hyde Park," he continued in a wheedling tone. "You would love to see the fashionable set there, I am sure."

"I really think I had best not, Cousin," she returned weakly, dropping her eyes. She knew his mother was not above issuing a direct command where her son's pleasures were concerned, and she waited nervously for the directive to come.

"Selinda," Aunt Prudence began, fixing the girl with a chilling stare. Selinda steeled herself. "I believe you are looking somewhat pale. I think perhaps it would be wisest if you kept to your chamber for the remainder of the day."

Seizing on this opportunity, Selinda immediately excused herself, leaving Rupert and his mother exchanging wrathful glances.

"That is really above everything, Mater," he fumed. "I told you I'd brook no interference and I shall not. I believe if you were wise you would allow me my way in this one thing."

"And I believe if *you* were wise," his mother returned in soft, dangerous tones, "you would not meddle in matters that cannot but harm you. You have led a soft life, Rupert. I would not test the patience of one who has not."

At that, Rupert threw down his serviette pettishly and exited with what he fondly believed was a dignified silence, although his weighty tread rattled the serving pieces on the sideboard. His mother sat for a time regarding the door through which he had withdrawn. It was clear the little minx had completely wormed her way into Rupert's affections and left no room for her. The way he fawned on the chit, bowing and scraping, made Prudence want to retch. She'd put a spoke in her son's wheels soon enough, she decided. They'd not stay a moment longer than they had to at Harroweby House—and there'd be no returning either. Rupert could cast sullen looks all he wanted, but they'd set sail as soon as ever might be.

In fact, she could think of no reason to delay their departure until tomorrow. Thanks to her efforts of the previous evening, her own preparations were in order. All sewn up, she thought with a grim smile. Yes, with a little concentrated effort, they could be gone by this afternoon and never see the noxious chit again. But she must be certain to dash off a note to that insect, Basham, to apprise him of her sudden departure. Unfortunately, the legalities surrounding the sale of Darrowdean necessitated his inclusion in that aspect of her plan.

Prudence pulled herself up from the breakfast table, stopped at the sideboard, and stuffed one last sausage into her mouth for good measure. She had a strenuous day ahead of her and needed to maintain her strength. As she passed through the foyer, the door knocker sounded. As usual, the butler was nowhere in sight. Much put upon, she sighed heavily and threw the door open. On the doorstep stood two gentlemen whom she thought she recognized from Selinda's ball. One was certainly that Lord Waverly, an odd volume if half the stories about him were true. It seemed, after all, as if Rupert's fears might have had some merit. This interest would have to be nipped in the bud.

Before the gentlemen could even hand her their cards, she summoned up an alarming expression and announced, "We are under quarantine here, gentlemen. Typhus. If you value your health, you'd best be off and good day to you." With that she slammed the door in their faces.

"I say, Waverly," Bastion began with an eloquent shudder, "could that have been a sausage in her hand?"

"I sincerely hope so," his cousin replied, grimacing at the memory of her greasy mouth and fingers, "considering the alternatives."

"Havey-cavey if you ask me."

"I bow to your superior judgment in those matters," Waverly remarked absently, his concentration focused on what appeared to be the dim possibility of ever being admitted to the presence of Lady Selinda.

"You don't suppose they've really got the fever there, do you?"

"I would consider it highly unlikely." Waverly glanced up at the window Lucy had indicated to him the day before. No vase of flowers was visible.

"Not but what I don't appreciate your efforts to secure my future, Roland, but it don't seem like we're making much headway, and from the looks

146

of the chief Gorgon, it don't look as if we're likely to."

"Never fear," Waverly replied, more to himself than his cousin, "I shan't give up hope yet. Perhaps we'll try again later in the day."

Lucy and Selinda were sitting quietly in their stark chamber, each occupied with her own thoughts but pretending to read, when Aunt Prudence unceremoniously burst in followed by Miss Snypish.

"Put on your pelisse, child, and be quick about it. Where is her valise, Snypish?"

The companion lost no time in pulling that item from the armoire and set about filling it, the scantiness of Lucy's wardrobe presenting a simple task.

"Whatever is going on, Aunt Prudence?" Selinda asked, suddenly stricken with a sickening fear. "You promised that Lucy and I would not be separated."

"Don't be hen-witted. I am merely taking Lucy on a short journey with me. It is a fine opportunity for one so young, although I have little hope she'll thank me for it. Stop looking like a gaping carp, brat, and help Miss Snypish with the packing." With that, she turned abruptly and left the room, Selinda following on her heels.

Lucy, who had been feeling uneasy all morning, now knew why. She immediately ran to the window and set the asters on the sill, thankful she'd had the foresight to have the vase in readiness. Then, with not the least intention of

147

aiding Miss Snypish's efforts, she ran from the room, intent on the gallery.

Miss Snypish had not been unaware of the child's mysterious action. That was a sly one and no mistake. She'd no idea, of course, why Lucy had taken the trouble to put the vase in the window, but she was not about to ignore her instincts. Quickly crossing to it, she picked up the flowers and tossed them out the window.

In the foyer, servants were busily removing Prudence's various trunks and hatboxes to the waiting carriage and Rupert was standing about glumly with his hands pushed into his pockets feeling as useless as ever he might. He wished he might take some sort of action to forestall the precipitous events going on about him but knew not how. Whatever had gotten his cross-grained beast of a mother into such an enormous pet anyway that they must suddenly leave today instead of tomorrow? Now the chance to pretty up to Selinda would have to wait until their return. He thought briefly of sending her some sort of letter but quickly decided that might be too easily intercepted. Above all things, he knew he must keep his intentions as close as possible.

He watched as Miss Snypish made her way down the stairs and handed a small valise to a footman with a look of decided satisfaction emblazoned across her face. He didn't at all like what he saw. Something more was going on than met the eye and he had no way of finding out what.

\*　　　\*　　　\*

148

Upon finding Lady Sybil in her customary retreat, Lucy heaved a sigh of relief. She quickly apprised the ghost of the plans for her sudden remove and concluded with a wry smile, "There is nothing for it but to be brave, I suppose, and hope for the best. Take care of Selinda for me."

"I have no intention of letting you go by yourself, child."

"But, Lady Sybil, even if you might, how could I rest easy leaving Selinda all alone?"

"In the first place," the ghost said gently, "you forget that the persons who offer the most threat are going along with you, my dear. You have more need of protection than your sister."

Lucy gulped, but said nothing.

"Secondly," the ghost went on, "you seem to be the only one who can see or hear me in any case, so I suspect my presence would be of little value here."

Lucy paced a bit, biting her lower lip before demanding, "But I still do not see how you can possibly follow me. I don't know of anything of yours I can take with me and I must be back downstairs before too much more time has passed. I dare not anger them now."

"Well," Lady Sybil explained, "I shall not be precisely following *you*. That disreputable woman has appropriated a favorite keepsake of mine which I had much rather you or your sister received. She is wearing it even as we speak. Never fear. As long as you are with her, I shall be with you."

* * *

When Lucy finally made her way downstairs, she found Prudence impatiently waiting for her. Selinda restrained the tears she felt pricking at her eyes and, in spite of the hand print glowing on one side of her face, smiled bravely at Lucy. Her protests had met only with unveiled threats as to what sort of treatment Lucy might expect if Selinda did not hold her peace. She gathered her little sister up into a silent embrace which Lucy returned with a violent energy. "Do not worry about me, Selinda," she managed to whisper. "There is a friend coming along with me I can rely on. And you—the best thing is you may rely on Lord Waverly!"

"But what can you possibly know of . . . ?"

"Do take care of yourself, Selinda," the child whispered, as she gave her sister one last squeeze.

These remarks had barely time to register on Selinda before Prudence snatched Lucy away by her collar and half-led, half-pulled her out to the carriage which was waiting in the rain. Selinda ran forward, but Rupert put himself in her way.

"Never fear. We shall return before long, little cousin," he said in a placatory tone. Selinda cast a sulphurous glance at him. Then with sudden inspiration he went on, "I assure you, all shall be well in the end, my dear. What's more, I shall make it my responsibility to look after the child."

"See that you do," Selinda told him through clenched teeth. "Believe me, I shall see you all dead if any harm comes to her."

Rupert's eyes widened, and he backed away. What monsters women were after all! There was not one of his acquaintance who wouldn't skewer a fellow the first time he crossed her will.

When the carriage finally rattled away, Selinda watched until it disappeared, then turned dejectedly into the house, tears of frustration and fear running down her cheeks. She had not the least idea what Lucy's cryptic message about some mysterious friend had meant and hardly dared hope there was any truth to it. The reference to Lord Waverly was more baffling still. She knew she had never mentioned his name to the child and could not think of any other person who might have. Selinda knew from long experience, however, that Lucy's odd ways were more often to be trusted than not; aiming a heartfelt petition at the heavens, she prayed that no harm would come of this day's events.

These ruminations were interrupted by Miss Snypish who seemed all in a flutter. "Take this note round to Madame Claire's," she was instructing a footman, "and be quick about it. Now, Lady Selinda, pray accompany me to my rooms that you may advise me on my toilette."

"Miss Snypish," Selinda ventured, her voice trembling faintly, "I am much distressed by what has just passed, and my aunt has refused me any explanation whatsoever. I do not know where my sister has been taken nor for how long."

"Do not trouble yourself," she was told shortly. "Your aunt merely desired some companionship for her journey. And, I am sure, some carrying and fetching as I am not to go along."

"But Aunt Prudence despises Lucy!"

"Well," Miss Snypish continued grimly, "let us hope that the child does nothing to provoke her. Come along now."

After receiving a strict admonition to cease her moping, Selinda trailed up the stairs after Miss Snypish, her heart a stony lump. She had never thought that a respite from her aunt and cousin could possibly leave her with such feelings of torment. And yet, she realized, their absence quite possibly offered her the only opportunity she might have to amend the wretched situation in which she and her sister were trapped. If she could elude Miss Snypish even for an afternoon, she might be able to manage events to some conclusion.

There was to be no chance for such an excursion that day, however, for Selinda was immediately pulled into Miss Snypish's chamber (which, she noticed, was much more elegantly appointed than her own) and immediately imposed upon to arrange the companion's lank tresses in a more becoming style. Selinda set about this demeaning occupation with little argument, for she knew that would achieve nothing. Indeed, the past six months had so accustomed her to performing tasks beneath her station that the impropriety of such an endeavor barely registered.

As Miss Snypish's dull, limp locks slipped stubbornly through various combinations of combs and pins, Selinda frowned, trying desperately to think of some course of action that might be open to her. She and Lucy had often argued about the wisdom of seeking out Mr. Basham for a private conversation if such a thing could be arranged. Lucy had, for some reason, been dead set against it. Yet, Selinda knew that to seek out any other party would prove fruitless, for Basham had been named executor of the estate.

If only she might depend on Lucy's cryptic comment about Lord Waverly! Selinda felt in her heart that he was the very sort of person from whom she might obtain good advice. There was something very odd about his marked attentions toward Miss Snypish, but perhaps she had judged him too quickly. Certainly that regard had served to deflect Miss Snypish's waspish temper, and for that she was duly grateful. Her attention now returned to that creature whose appearance was not a bit improved by Selinda's ministrations.

"I believe there is nothing for it but pomade," Selinda remarked with a less-than-hopeful sigh.

With that, she was directed to the bundle of goods purchased the day before at Cosgrove's and found there a jar of the stuff that smelled very much like axle grease mixed with violets and was of a similar consistency. It did the trick, however, and soon Miss Snypish's hair was piled in an odd, inflexible arrangement just above her ears. Selinda pushed at it a bit longer, wondering if perhaps she hadn't used too much of the stuff, but it would not budge.

"I would not have believed it possible," Miss Snypish murmured.

Selinda bit her lip, wondering what new trial she must face, watching with morbid fascination as the coiffure set to dull opacity. "Truly, Miss

Snypish," she began hesitantly, "I am sure with practice I might do better, but I have never before attempted such an endeavor . . ."

"Then you are to be congratulated," she was told, much to her surprise. "Who would have thought you would be possessed of a talent? Now you may leave me. I suspect we may have callers this afternoon, by the way, so prepare yourself for company."

As she departed, Selinda could not help but dart a curious glance over her shoulder at Miss Snypish, who sat before her glass, rapt with self-admiration.

# Chapter Fifteen

Lord Waverly and his cousin called once again at Harroweby House later that afternoon. The weather had cleared a little, and the two gentlemen stood on the stoop for some minutes in conversation before applying once again for admission.

"Now you are certain you have the drill straight, Bastion?"

"I am not such a nodcock that I cannot follow a simple line of reasoning. I only hope you are correct. Odious as I am certain it will be, I shall steel myself to doing the pretty with that Friday-faced companion. You're certain there is no other way to Lady Selinda?"

"You've seen yourself how she's watched," Lord Waverly reminded him. "Trust me, Miss Snypish is the chink in the armor. I suppose it's asking too much to expect you should be grateful that I interest myself in your affairs. You surely cannot imagine I find this sort of endeavor at all diverting."

"Oh, nothing of the kind," his cousin reassured him quickly. "It's just that I had rather we approached it the other way around."

"I thought I had explained my plan sufficiently. If your reputation were not rivaling Byron's for profligacy, there would be no trouble with your approaching an innocent miss in her first season. But as it stands, any guardian would as soon cast their charge to a crocodile. You must therefore convince the companion of your honorable character before you begin to even hint at your intentions. She's an odd touch, this Miss Snypish, but she'll be a friend to your suit if you can ingratiate yourself."

"I only hope you do not expect me to escort her any place I am likely to be known," Bastion huffed. "I should never live it down!"

"I hardly think it likely we shall be visiting any of the hells you are known to frequent," Waverly told him crushingly.

The marquess bit back the retort that rose to his lips. He was, after all, determined to give his cousin's scheme a try, for the least of the benefits that might be derived from it was the winning of his wager with Slaverington. A hundred pounds, after all, was nothing to sneeze at to someone whose pockets were so constantly to let as his. However, if he played his cards right, he might well land himself in the middle of a plum pudding. For now he'd ignore the heiress and court the shrew, but before long, he promised himself, he would set about a scheme of his own—if only he could think of one.

At this moment, Waverly's eye was caught by a

flash of yellow in the boxwood that grew by the front door. On closer inspection, he was alarmed to find some seven or eight of Lucy's asters scattered through the shrubbery. Clearly they had fallen from one of the windows above, for none was growing near. As soon as possible he must find out what had occasioned Lucy's distress.

When at last the door knocker was applied, both gentlemen were surprised to find themselves admitted by the butler and ushered into the presence of the ladies. The changes that had been wrought in Miss Snypish were nothing short of remarkable. Her new coiffure added not only some six inches to her height but a startling gleam now shone in her predatory eye. Moreover, Miss Motley, working with the promise of a considerable bonus, had been able to deliver one of the new gowns, a walking dress made up in the apple green cambric, abundantly trimmed with corbeau ribbons. Selinda, in a plain gray poplin, was happy enough to fade into the shadows.

"My dear Lord Waverly," Miss Snypish gushed as she came forward to take his hand, "such a pleasant surprise. Lady Selinda and I are quite wasting away with ennui."

At this uncharacteristic speech, Selinda started in some amazement and would have been further surprised to have discovered the truth which lay behind it. Miss Snypish, feeling that her entrée into polite society called for more than a surface polish, had been peeping into the pages of a stylish novel to discover another mode of address than that which she typically employed. She had only been able to find a very few phrases which might suit her purposes, but she was determined to employ them as often as possible.

"Miss Snypish, I must say you are looking quite a new person. My compliments." Waverly bowed briefly over her hand before nodding to Selinda. "Now ladies, you must do me the honor of permitting me to make my cousin known to you." As he made this presentation, Waverly was gratified to see that at least Miss Snypish's altered looks stole the marquess's attention from Lady Selinda. Indeed, his cousin seemed to regard the gaunt companion with the same hypnotic fascination as a doomed mouse displayed before a hooded cobra.

"Shall we drive out?" Waverly asked. "The weather seems to be holding for a bit. Even so, I imagine we shall have the park quite to ourselves."

This last was to reassure his cousin for whom Waverly was beginning to have some sympathy. That Miss Snypish was certainly a repellant creature! True, Bastion richly deserved to make some sort of recompense for the years of trouble he had caused, but after all, it was not as if the fellow had ever committed a capital offense.

"We shall be delighted," Miss Snypish answered for them all, and, commandeering Bastion's arm, led the way to the waiting carriage.

The park was quite deserted, as Waverly had predicted, but even so, Bastion soon suggested that they alight from their conveyance and seek out a likely pathway. There, he hoped, they would be even less likely to draw attention to themselves. Before long, the two couples were strolling along well-maintained gravel paths at some distance from each other.

The rainfall had hastened the falling of the autumn leaves and it now seemed to Selinda as if they were walking through a golden blizzard. She had always found autumn to be a melancholy time of year and was doubly affected by it today, so anxious was she about the well-being of her little sister. She had been trying all afternoon to reassure herself, but with little success. It was all she could do to maintain a tranquil demeanor.

Waverly had not been insensible to her distress. The sight of Lucy's scattered asters had prompted an intense disquiet which Lady Selinda's wan appearance did nothing to allay. Thus far she had said absolutely nothing, but her silent anguish spoke far more eloquently than any amount of tearful ravings might have done. What, he wondered anxiously, had transpired since his last visit with Lucy? He wondered if the child's eavesdropping had been discovered and whether she had even been able to convey its import to her sister. He cursed himself as a wretched incompetent, for it was clear that something untoward had taken place in spite of his assumption that everything was under control.

He had already contacted his man of business and described the tangle in which Lady Selinda and her sister found themselves. Although Mr. Noon was often irritatingly efficient and painstaking, Waverly knew he had but to bring a difficulty to the man's attention and all aspects of its resolution would be attended to. As he watched his cousin and Miss Snypish round a bend in the pathway, he drew Lady Selinda aside to a small copse. There, he laid his greatcoat over a damp stone bench where they sat quietly for a moment.

"Lord, Waverly, I . . ." Selinda began, then stopped short. She had, for a fraction of a second, considered drawing off her gloves and fluttering her eyelashes; there, she had often been assured by a series of governesses, lay the path to certain destruction, and she knew she must take some sort of action. However, even Selinda knew there was hardly time to bring about a seduction. The place was all wrong, too, she supposed, for it was not even moonlit. Even though images from last night's shocking dream flitted through her head, she decided instead to rely on Lucy's recommendation to trust his Lordship; the only difficulty was in forming the proper words.

"Yes, Lady Selinda?"

"It's very odd, but my sister said I might . . ." Here she faltered again. However could she explain her peculiar reliance on the judgment of a mere child?

Waverly smiled encouragingly. "Lady Lucy is a great favorite of mine. You are fortunate to have her."

Although these unlooked-for words went a good way to reassuring her, Selinda's lower lip began to tremble. "I am afraid, Lord Waverly that I do not have her at all. Oh! It has been the most horrid day!"

Even though Selinda had neither removed her gloves nor fluttered her eyelashes, Lord Waverly was suddenly moved to take her into his arms and pat her back, whispering nothing more romantic

160

than, "There, there, Lady Selinda. There, there."

Selinda sighed raggedly and surrendered to the embrace. Even though it was nothing like her dream, it felt so good, after all her trials, to finally be comforted, to rest in strong arms, and to feel for a moment, however brief, that someone else might undertake to shoulder her burdens.

They continued in this fashion for some minutes until Selinda, sensible that such an arrangement would not at all meet with Miss Snypish's approval should she and the marquess suddenly come upon them, reluctantly pulled herself from Waverly's arms.

"Now tell me all, madam," Waverly said, taking her small hands into his. "I spied Lucy's distress signal when we arrived just now—would that I had seen it sooner!—so I know that something disagreeable must have happened. But trust me and we shall contrive somehow to make everything right."

"Lucy's distress signal?" she asked, greatly puzzled.

"She did not tell you? Has she told you anything of what went on yesterday?"

"Not a thing," Selinda told him, her eyes wide.

"I suppose I am not surprised. She is a remarkable child, but I imagine she takes too much on herself. I am sure she felt that you already bore a sufficient burden without hearing further unsavory revelations."

As Waverly went on to explain the import of his outing with Lucy, the whole horrid picture came into crystalline focus for Selinda. How could Lucy have kept this intelligence from her? Much of it

Selinda had suspected, but the extent of her supposed relations' corruption shocked her beyond words. The very idea than anyone should prey on orphans offended every sensibility. Like Lucy, however, her greatest distress was occasioned by the thought of losing her home, and she was exceedingly grateful to hear the measures Lord Waverly had already taken.

"Now," he want on, "tell me what distressed Lucy into displaying her yellow asters."

"Oh, sir, they have taken my Lucy away and I fear without the constraint of my presence she shall be cuffed about unmercifully, for the poor child does seem to put their backs up. I am a little heartened to learn they must have taken her to Darrowdean while they transact the sale, but now I am afraid they will be tempted to flee once that is done. Will they force her to go with them or abandon her along the way?"

Waverly sat in thought for a moment before speaking. "I fear there is nothing for it but to go to Darrowdean as quickly as possible. You wish to come along with me, don't you?"

"Of course, but however shall I get away?"

"I shall leave you instructions in Lucy's pouch tonight at midnight. Do you think you will be able to go out?"

"Miss Snypish retires quite early, and I don't imagine the servants will stir themselves. I'm sure I can do it. What then?"

"Why we shall abduct Lucy, of course," he smiled as he pressed her hand. "I'm sure she will think it great fun."

# Chapter Fifteen

As the Marquess of Bastion and Miss Snypish threaded the tree-lined lanes, the latter's face all but glowed with excitement. The marquess was everything she had hoped he might be: titled (of course), handsome (to her way of thinking), and as malleable as potter's clay. Nothing could be better! She had, at first, been by no means encouraged that so much of his conversation seemed to lead back to the subject of Lady Selinda Harroweby, but, if he were indeed the shy person his cousin Waverly had described, it stood to reason he would fall back on a subject he supposed to be neutral. For safety's sake, however, Miss Snypish had fed him a Banbury tale about Lady Selinda which had seemed to dampen his interest quickly enough. Indeed, the heart-rending tale of Lady Selinda's failing health seemed to have set an expression of decided consternation on the marquess's ordinarily bland face.

Anxious to further draw Bastion's attention to

her own charms instead, Miss Snypish went on to describe in no small detail her recent forays into the stock market, and she was gratified to see his interest immediately riveted at the mention of money. Her dealings had, in fact, been a source of secret pride to her. Because of her oddly situated employment (in which silent complicity paid a good deal more than mere competence ever had) she had, by her standards, a goodly amount of capital at her disposal.

As she described the workings of the market, the Marquess of Bastion had been instantly impressed with this undertaking's resemblance to the games of chance which had both fascinated and frustrated him over the years. Could it be that faro and finance had something in common? Enthralled, he questioned her closely about the various subtleties of her investments.

"Why, it sounds exactly like something one might come across at Boodle's or White's," Bastion murmured, awestruck at the notion. "And you say you actually profit from this endeavor?"

"Consistently," Miss Snypish assured him with a proud nod, "for it really is more than gambling. You see, an investment is nothing more than a wager that the value of a commodity, for example, will increase. However, it is a good deal more like placing money on a horse, I should imagine, than wagering on a toss of the dice. *That* is ruled by chance alone, of course. With a horse, however, I daresay you must know something of its lineage and past performance. You have information which enables you to make an informed wager."

Bastion allowed, with growing respect for the lady, that this was quite true.

"Well, it is just so on the 'change," she explained earnestly. "One knows a certain amount about the market, the tenor of the times, the past performance of the commodity. It's all in the newspapers if one but looks. It's quite simple, really. In fact," she went on in a conspiratorial tone, "I have quite a nest egg saved up myself. I shall be glad to let you know of any investments I make."

"I say!" he exclaimed with some feeling. "That's very sporting of you, I must say, Miss Snypish. There's some—most—who don't give a fig how I get on. You truly are a remarkable woman!"

Miss Snypish all but blushed with pleasure at this first compliment of her adult life. Yes, she would snare this prize, she told herself with resolute conviction, or die trying.

When the fascinated pair at last rejoined Lord Waverly and Selinda, Miss Snypish wore a look of marked triumph. She had held high hopes for this meeting, but, when it came right down to it, she had not actually dreamed that engaging the marquess's attention would prove to be so easy. Moreover, in a very brief time, she had been able to discover yet another interest she and that gentleman held in common. Immediately, she announced the plans for the following day.

"We shall all," she informed the group in tones

that forbade anything like dissension, "visit Madame Tussaud's Waxworks on the morrow. That remarkable lady has just brought a new exhibition to town, Lord Bastion has told me, and I am most anxious to see it. I have heard," she went on in a gleeful undertone, "that she uses actual human teeth! I cannot wait."

"It really is the most amazing thing, Waverly," his cousin told him with considerable enthusiasm. "I saw it last year with Slaverington. Some don't care for it, but I must admit I found it quite fascinating. Exceedingly enlightening."

The marquess now cast a sidelong glance at Lady Selinda. He had noticed on his first seeing her that day that she was not at all in looks; at this last description of Madame Tussaud's artistic technique, however, she had become pale, indeed. How could he have ever thought her a beauty? he wondered with incredulity. It must surely have been all the champagne he had drunk the night of her ball, he decided with a frown. And then, there was also that hereditary wasting sickness of which that extraordinary Miss Snypish had so kindly warned him. She was right it seemed: the disease's course must be extremely rapid, for the girl looked a good deal less robust than she had just a week ago. *Bed her or wed her . . .* The terms of his wager with Slaverington echoed in his head.

Marrying the poor chit would not be such a bad thing, he supposed, and the prospect of inheriting her fortune more quickly than he had imagined was a fair inducement. But bedding her and casting her aside? That was something else entirely,

166

wasn't it? He was well-aware that his reputation was not quite what it ought to be, but even *he* wasn't equal to fulfilling his wager by such an expedient. Would Slaverington allow him to cry off he wondered?

As the carriage rattled along, Lucy shrank into the squabs, trying to make her diminutive presence even less noticeable. Sharing the compartment with persons of such immense proportions as Rupert and his mother was not a pretty prospect, even for one so small as Lucy. Each took up the greater part of the bench upon which they had deposited themselves, and the child was in a quandary to decide which of them should have the bliss of squashing her up against the door. Furthermore, neither scoundrel was in charity with the other, and Lucy suspected that it would not be long before their interchange of barbed glances became verbal. All she could do, however, was envy Lady Sybil's invisibility.

In spite of enormous discomfort, emotional and physical, the long coach ride to Darrowdean still held some small amusement for Lucy. To begin with, it took a fair amount of concentration for her to maintain a sober countenance. Although Lucy was, of course, the only passenger who could either see or hear the ghost, Lady Sybil carried on a continuous monologue, reminiscing about the various sights of London as their carriage made its way through the city, remarking on the countryside and villages through which they passed, and, from time to time, commenting satirically on Prudence and her unlovable son in the most outrageous terms imaginable.

Beyond this, however, the irreverent spirit further diverted herself by plaguing their dreams whenever either Prudence or Rupert chanced to drift off to sleep. Even though the sight of their disconcerted faces as they started into wakefulness was extremely amusing, Lucy had much rather the ghost allowed them their repose, for it was a good deal less noxious for her than the strained vigilance that followed their dreams.

Lucy sat, therefore, biting the insides of her cheeks to keep from laughing aloud for several hours, until the rattling carriage came to halt in front of an inn. Rupert's stomach had been rumbling unmercifully for some hours, but his mother, who had put away a meal of Amazon proportions that morning, had insisted they wait until late afternoon to break their fast. The pair descended the carriage heavily, snapping irritably at one another. Lucy waited a moment for the vehicle to stop rocking before she attempted to follow them, but, as she moved forward, her progress was immediately obstructed by the substantial form of Rupert's mother.

"Stay in the coach, brat, and do not think of stirring," she was told crossly. "Don't for a moment think I haven't seen your sly little smirks. When you can behave yourself as a decent child ought, you shall be fed something. But not before."

With that, Prudence made her bulky way toward

the mouth-watering aromas issuing from the inn, and Lady Sybil, perforce, followed in her wake. If only the wretched woman had put the pomander into her luggage instead of insisting on constantly wearing it, the ghost might have been able to stay behind with Lucy. In addition to feeling that the child might need some reassurance, Lady Sybil had no desire to observe Prudence when she applied herself to her dinner. Something would have to be done about this inconvenience before too long, Lady Sybil decided.

Although Rupert was very nearly beside himself with hunger, he tarried a moment at the carriage door. He did not, of course, have any natural feeling for the child, but he did recognize an opportunity to ingratiate himself with Selinda. If he could pose as the brat's champion, he reasonsed, he might well find it an advantageous avenue into her older sister's heart once more. When the coachman, too, had made his way toward the taproom (Rupert trusted no one), he leaned in close and smiled.

"Never worry, dearest Lucy," he told her in a conspiratorial undertone. "I have promised your sister I shall look after you. I will see to it that you do not starve."

Quickly then, he followed his mother's retreating bulk and disappeared into the inn. A few moments later, he returned with several withered apples and the dry end of a loaf. "This was all I could contrive under that vulture's watchful eye," he whispered quickly, looking nervously over his shoulder. "Eat it all quickly and don't leave any cores about. It would benefit neither of us to be found out."

With that he hastily made his way back to the inn, leaving Lucy to munch away at her meager repast in peace. It would simply have to do until they reached their inn later on tonight, she told herself stoutheartedly. Surely, by then, Prudence would have relented somewhat. Or perhaps her small sins would be overshadowed by some offense of Rupert's. At least, Lucy hoped so.

When at last her guardians did return to the carriage, they moved with a sluggish waddle that bespoke their prowess at the table. As they settled once more into the squabs and their eyes grew heavy, Lucy darted a significant glance at Lady Sybil who graciously allowed them their sleep for the present. It was not long before their snores filled the compartment's air with a sonorous sawing.

In this relative tranquility, Lucy turned her thoughts to her predicament, steeling herself to the chilly dread now working away at her heart. Her resources were few, but better than they might have been. Lady Sybil was at her side most of the time, and, tied in a handkerchief in her pocket, she had the gold pieces Lord Waverly had left for her. Moreover, they were headed for Darrowdean. So, she had resources, a friend, and knew the territory. It could have been, she knew quite well, far, far worse.

As soon as Selinda and Miss Snypish had bid

farewell to their callers, the latter at once set about determining a costume for the morrow's expedition. Fortuitously, the companion did not call upon Selinda to assist her in this endeavor but left her to explore her own thoughts for the first time that day. These were, naturally, a good deal lighter than they had been two hours earlier or, indeed, for a good many months. It seemed altogether too good to credit that such a one as Lord Waverly was not only intimately acquainted with their horrid predicament, but had pledged his assistance as well.

As the elder of the sisters, Selinda had, for the most part, suffered their troubles as her own particular burden. Lucy, of course, was privy to their nature, but how could a mere child be expected to help, after all? Ironically, now that Lord Waverly had revealed the substance of Lucy's investigation, Selinda felt quite useless in comparison. Her little sister had been more successful in her endeavors than any might ever have guessed—infinitely more so than Selinda herself had been. It was altogether remarkable that the child had managed to learn (and to accomplish with that knowledge) so much in so short a time. It was not that Selinda was ungrateful—quite the reverse, in fact. But she did so wish that she might have saved Lucy's innocent childhood from the ravages it had lately undergone. Thanks to the child's efforts, however, the riddle of their supposed guardians' relationship was now unraveled and the aid of the inestimable Lord Waverly had been enlisted.

Lord Waverly! Selinda's ruminations were

brought to a sudden halt as she recalled the feeling of his arms around her that afternoon. That moment of comfort had been too brief, but it had been sufficient to still her fears and inexorably engage her heart. If only he could hold her forever! It had been more than just an embrace, of course, lovely as that instant had been. His proposed rescue of Lucy and his assumption of her own inclusion in the undertaking had completely overwhelmed her. How many other gentlemen, for all their lovely speeches, would do as much? They would be full of their protestations for her reputation and safety. They would very likely insist that sitting about in a fretful stew constituted a more proper show of sisterly concern than riding to poor Lucy's rescue. Ignorant cattle! There was now not the least doubt in Selinda's mind: she loved Lord Waverly and loved him completely. She would marry him and they could all live happily—

Just then, an exceedingly dampening thought occurred to her. The same set of events that promised to deliver the sisters from their distress brought with them yet another dilemma. It was quite clear now that Selinda need not embark on a precipitous marriage to anyone in order to bring about a change of fortune. In fact, she need not seduce Lord Waverly after all! Drat!

Suddenly, her newfound sense of deliverance clouded over with a despondency which made Selinda quite angry with herself. How could she wallow in such self-indulgent self-pity at such a time as this? Determinedly, she pulled herself from her brooding and forced herself to set about her business. Too much was at stake to cater to her own selfish ends.

The first thing Selinda did was to find her way around to the back of Harroweby House and ascertain the exact location of the pouch in which she would find Lord Waverly's missive at midnight. She knew quite well that such a nocturnal excursion would be regarded with suspicion should anyone notice her, and she did not wish to compound the probability of discovery by blundering about in complete darkness looking for the thing. Fortunately she was able to locate the little pouch after only a few minutes of searching through the ivy.

She had wondered whether she might write a short note of gratitude and enclose it therein, but immediately thought better of it. All of their plans would be foiled if that serpent Miss Snypish should have the least suspicion of them. Even though that person had treated her with unusual civility of late, comparatively speaking, Selinda also knew that, just beneath her veneer, rested the same obdurate heart of their earlier acquaintance. She knew she dared not test it.

On her way back to the house, Selinda prepared herself to make the same journey hampered by cover of darkness. She counted the number of steps it would take for her to reach the garden wall from the door by which she would exit the house, then, through each room she must pass, and last, the number of stairs she must descend. It would not do at all, she reminded herself wryly, for her midnight excursion to be punctuated by the sounds of breaking glass and muffled oaths. This task accomplished, she repaired to her chamber to assemble such items as might be useful on the journey to Darrowdean.

That evening she shared a quiet dinner with Miss Snypish who, taking advantage of her employers' absence, had dispensed with the services of their all-too-mediocre cook and sent out for a repast prepared by the chef at The Clarendon. Selinda was a little surprised at having been invited to partake of this extravagant treat until she recollected that, to Miss Snypish's ostentatious notions, solitary splendor was no splendor at all.

It was a vastly different sort of meal from those to which Selinda had been accustomed of late. Although she had had little appetite for the ample but bland dishes served up by their current staff, she felt her mouth water as she regarded the richly laden table: there was a steaming ham pudding, curry of rabbit, buttered lobster, artichoke bottoms, and vegetable tart, as well as a fruited syllabub and several custard creams. Miss Snypish had also called for a bottle of champagne from the cellar.

Knowing that she would be needing every ounce of strength in the days ahead, Selinda applied herself to the repast with unusual dedication; however, she soon discovered that she was no match for her dinner partner. Selinda watched in silent fascination as Miss Snypish demolished plate after laden plate. Even a hollow leg would not explain that sort of capacity, she reflected with wide-eyed bewilderment.

As if reading the girl's thoughts, Miss Snypish commented briefly, "I believe I should do much better if my form were a trifle more filled out."

Selinda, refraining from any sort of appraisal of the companion's sparsely set bones, quietly allowed that such a repast as this evening's would very likely be efficacious toward that end.

"That is quite what I thought," Miss Snypish pronounced, availing herself, much to Selinda's disbelief, to another helping of the artichoke bottoms. This she dispatched with amazing rapidity; then, wiping her chin, she slowly arose. "I shall be sleeping late in the morning, so see that you do not disturb me." With that, Miss Snypish exited the dining room and made her way to her chamber where she looked forward to applying a generous amount of oil of talc to her sallow complexion.

Selinda still had several hours to wait before she could venture out into the garden to find Waverly's message, but she dared not allow herself to fall asleep for fear of missing the appointed hour altogether. Taking a branch of candles from the sideboard, she repaired to the library in hopes of finding a book in which she might immerse herself until that time. Oddly enough, for all her troubles, she found her mind returning from time to time to the little novel she and Lucy had been reading just last week. It must still be in Lord Waverly's possession. Ah, the romantic travails of

Rosamonde and Roderick! How, she wondered, had it all turned out?

Because of Prudence's penurious habits, Selinda found the library almost unbearably chilly, and she immediately set about kindling a small fire. There were already several partially burned fagots which would serve as a good foundation, and she knelt to add a few more pieces of firewood. In among the logs, there were also several charred pieces of paper, and, as she reached her taper in to reignite them, she suddenly stopped as she recognized Prudence's spidery hand. Carefully she drew the pages out one by one and spread them before her on the hearth. Some of these, she was interested to see, were still quite legible.

After a few moments, Selinda sat back on her knees and bit her lower lip. Unfortunately the greater part of the documents appeared to be in some sort of code; even though she could read individual words, little of it made any sense. Holding up her branch of candles, she examined each piece of paper again. All at once her eye was captured by one page in particular. On it she could clearly read her sister's name.

Holding back her excitement, she carefully carried the page over to the desk where she could more easily examine it. Although roughly half of the page had been destroyed and much of what remained had been crossed out, Selinda was able to decipher enough to determine that the document was a draft of a letter to Mr. Basham. For the most part, the message appeared to consist primarily of details concerning the remove to Darrowdean, the status of the sale, and the woman's sudden decision to bring the younger of the Harroweby sisters along with her. Suddenly, Selinda's eye was caught by a partial phrase, ". . . then dispose of the chi . . ." Immediately, her heart began to pound with fear, for she could only believe the last word must have been *child*.

What in God's name must possess the woman? Selinda raged inwardly. Neither she nor Lucy had done anything to harm Prudence, yet she planned not only to rob them blind but threaten their safety as well. Forcefully, it came to Selinda that she must not wait a moment to act. She was to check the pouch for Waverly's message at midnight, but she knew he must deliver it some time after darkness had fallen. If only he had not yet come by, she prayed, she might be able to catch him.

Carefully, she folded the partial letter and tucked it into her sleeve. Then she swept the rest of the charred papers back into the fireplace. She silently peeped out of the library door into the long, dim corridor. No one was about. Stepping from the room and shutting the door behind her, she then noiselessly made her way up the stairs and through the halls to her chamber, her heart beating with apprehension. Once there, she quickly donned a heavy wool cloak and changed from her worn slippers to sturdier shoes, for it was altogether possible that she might have a long wait in the cold darkness. Then she transferred the charred fragment of letter to her reticule and silently made her way out.

The house was still as she opened the door to

the garden, and the moonless night, damp with threatening rain, offered only the comfort of concealment. Holding her breath and carefully counting her steps, arms stretched out a little way before her, Selinda slowly approached the vine-covered pillars. The path seemed rougher than it had in the daylight, and it felt as if a long time had passed before she finally attained her goal. As her hands traced the line of the pillar, they finally found the little opening in which Lord Waverly's pouch had been secreted. Heart pounding, she opened the clasp. It was empty.

All would be well, she thought, allowing herself to breathe again. Lord Waverly had not yet arrived. When he did, she could tell him of her frightening discovery. He would know just what to do. In the darkness she shivered, wrapped the cloak more tightly about herself, and dropping to her knees, she leaned back against the pillar to wait.

# *Chapter Sixteen*

Whether Selinda had been awakened by the rain that was just beginning to fall or the sounds of footsteps near her in the darkness, she did not at first know. It took her a moment to pull herself from the sluggishness of sleep and realize where she was and why she felt so achey and miserable. Then she remembered.

"Lord Waverly?" she whispered tentatively.

There was a momentary hesitation and then a long sigh was audible to Selinda's ears. In the silence that followed, Selinda's heart began to pound as she realized she had, in all likelihood, spoken too soon. After all, who knew what sort of men (and how many of them!) loitered about in the darkness of such black nights as this. Anything might happen to her, and no one would be the wiser.

"I am Richard, Lord Waverly's man," a superior voice cut through the darkness at last. Sliding back the shield of his dark lantern a mere fraction of an inch so that only a slender beam of light escaped, the footman looked down disdainfully at Selinda's huddled and shivering form. "I had understood I was to convey this note to a *pouch*, not a *person*."

These words were delivered in tones of such icy disdain that Selinda was hard-pressed to gather her courage. Nevertheless, her situation was desperate. She swallowed hard and summoned her determination.

"You must take me to Lord Waverly at once," she told him quickly. "We have not a moment to lose."

Well, this was really beyond anything, Richard told himself. It was bad enough to be sent out into the damp and dark as if he were a mere errand boy, but he certainly was not in the habit of conveying females to his Lordship. He was paid far too much to stoop to that sort of thing. The lady's voice, however, told him she was quality, and he dared not disobey. He had witnessed his master's anger on only one other occasion (some silliness about the beating of a horse) but he preferred not to witness it again. Leading the way into the darkness and ungraciously forcing the lady to all but run to keep up with his stride, Richard once again considered the advantages of seeking employment elsewhere.

It was not more than a mile to Lord Waverly's residence, but the combined effects of rain falling ever more heavily, a rising wind, and the slippery cobblestones made Selinda even more cold and miserable than she had been during her vigil. Half an hour later, Richard was glad to deposit the now-sodden girl in his master's front hallway like a bundle of wet wash. Most of the lights had been extinguished, but the sounds of pacing issuing from Waverly's library bespoke that gentleman's anxiety as he awaited his servant's return. Richard left Selinda for a moment, scratched on the library door, and announced in his most contemptuous manner, "A *person* wishes to see you, my lord."

A bare moment later, Selinda found herself being borne in strong arms to the library, deposited carefully on a sofa in front of a roaring fire, and her wrists chafed by anxious hands. She blinked away the raindrops from her eyelashes and encountered the grave face of Lord Waverly.

"Some blankets, Richard, and be smart about it," Waverly commanded in a terrible voice. He had been struck to the core when he saw Selinda's pitiful form leaning against a wall for support in his own entryway. What a fool he'd been to send that useless Richard on so delicate a mission. Wretchedly, he looked into Selinda's pale face as a wave of guilt and apprehension washed over him.

Richard, daunted by his master's wrathful tone, quickly returned bearing an armful of blankets. Waverly had by now removed his own cravat and was wiping rain from the girl's face with it. He knew that she must eventually get out of those wet clothes, but, for now, she needed to be kept warm. Without ceremony, he relieved the footman of his burden and arranged the blankets over her, tucking them in well. This task accomplished, he turned and addressed the man.

"Well, Richard," he pronounced with a controlled iciness, "you may now explain why a hackney was not engaged."

Richard's chin tilted up just a fraction, and he held his employer's eye a moment before looking away. "It did not appear seemly to me, my lord," was his reply.

"And criminal negligence is more seemly? Idiot!" Waverly turned back to Selinda, who now, at least, was shivering less violently than before. Controlling himself with an effort, he continued, "Rouse Mrs. Fortnum and have a hot bath prepared in the blue room. Then you will wait until I call for you again."

By now Selinda had recovered sufficiently to look about her. Of all the rooms to which she might have been shown, the library spoke most compellingly of Lord Waverly's personality and tastes. Certainly, it bespoke comfort with its rich paneling and deep cushioned chairs and sofas. This was a room for living, not for show. Unlike many libraries, it actually looked as if it were used for reading. Many volumes, in fact, lay open on tables or were piled haphazardly about the room. Much to her chagrin, she noticed that one of these was the romance which had come into Lord Waverly's possession that fateful day—it must have been a hundred years ago! Catching the direction of her gaze, Waverly put the volume into her hand and quietly smiled down at her.

He said nothing of it (although Selinda was torn between wishing and dreading that he might) but poured a glass of brandy and brought it to her. "Try drinking some of this, Lady Selinda," he told her, his expression carefully unreadable as he looked at her. She had forgotten how very blue his eyes were. "It will make you feel a little warmer, you see."

Obediently, Selinda took a small sip, raised her eyebrows, and shook her head a little as she pulled back.

"I know it is not what you are accustomed to, Lady Selinda—I remember how you quite lost your heart to champagne—but you must take one more sip. Please. Then I shall allow you to tell me what brings you to risk your well-being on such a night as this. There, now."

Selinda swallowed once more and realized that this second taste was not nearly so bad as the first had been. She sipped again and felt the warmth course through her. Then, taking a deep breath, she began without preamble. "It's Lucy. I fear she is in even greater danger than I had ever imagined. We must set out directly to find her, sir."

Another gentleman might well have discounted the look of apprehension which overcast Selinda's features, might have chalked it up to female excitability or hyperbole.

"Tell me," was all Lord Waverly said.

By way of reply, Selinda pulled the remains of the charred letter from her reticule and watched breathlessly as the gentleman's features gradually became as grave as her own.

"I am afraid you may have the right of it, Lady Selinda," he said at last. "I shall go at once."

"And I shall go with you," Selinda told him resolutely. It was not a question.

"Lady Selinda . . ." he began hesitantly, as he took her hand in his and knelt beside her. Aside from concerns about her physical well-being after such a harrowing night, Lord Waverly had no objections to her accompanying him. In fact, he could think of nothing he would like better. However, he decided, it was high time he attempted to curb his eccentric outlook and had a care for the reputation of others. Richard's obvious conclusions about the nature of Selinda's visit had not been lost on him. He did not care one jot for the malicious whispering of the cats of the *ton*, but he knew he must protect Selinda. Silently, he cursed himself for a fool for ever suggesting that she might join him in his attempt to rescue Lucy. It was just that he had never been used to considering such matters before.

"Do not think to dissuade me," Selinda broke in on his deliberations. Seeking valiantly to suppress her shivers, she went on, "Oh, I know what you will say, and you are right in part. I am tired and cold and wet and very much distressed. But I shall be more than distressed if I am left behind; I shall be *distracted* if I am treated like a useless female. Now, I think we might just as well wait until it is light, for we shall need to get some rest if we are to be of use to anyone. By then my things will be dry. I believe the roads will be quite muddy, so we had best ride, don't you think? Have you such a thing as a sidesaddle about?"

When Selinda had finished her hurried little speech, she bit her lower lip and there rested in her eyes such a hopeful expression that Lord Waverly was, for a moment, quite unable to pronounce the objections which he had been formulating. After a time, however, he smiled, "My Lady Selinda, I know you are quite in earnest, but I feel enough of a rattle for having let Lucy down in this way. I will not on top of everything else be responsible for your becoming ill or—"

"But Lord Waverly," she interrupted him with a small smile, "you can have no notion of my constitution. I have never been sick a day in all my life and, even should I contract some chill or other, I do not imagine I shall die from it. On the other hand, should you be so rash as to leave me behind, I must give you fair warning—I shall somehow contrive to follow you on my own, and *that*, I am sure you will credit, would be far more disastrous. As for other considerations, they are my concern, not yours. I pray you do not think of them."

But Lord Waverly did think of them with unaccustomed dedication, and it did his newfound sense of propriety little credit that its preachments were punctuated with visions of taking Selinda once more into his arms and kissing her thoroughly.

Selinda's mind was similarly occupied. Why, she fretted inwardly, must she wait to be kissed? What would happen, she wondered, if she just reached her hand out and traced the line of his jaw? Or pulled his hand to her cheek? Just to let him know that this endeavor was one they shared together? Tentatively, she drew her hand out from under the blanket. He caught it in his and held it. Well . . . that was . . . acceptable. She frowned inwardly, suspecting that what she really wanted was to live her dream of the previous night. But, was that so bad? After all, she loved him. And the brandy had warmed her so delightfully. And he was so handsome. Well, then. She *would* kiss him.

She leaned in toward him just a fraction further. He smiled slowly and began to lower his face to hers. Just then, an insistent miaow broke the silence and a round orange kitten nimbly hopped up between them and began purring loudly about Selinda's face.

"Well!" she exclaimed with a short laugh as they drew apart. "Who's your fat friend?"

"You may well ask!" he replied ruefully, picking up the kitten and staring into its bright blue eyes. "This cream-swilling fellow doesn't seem to know where he's not wanted. Well, my lord Cat, you'd best make yourself scarce or I shall take you along on tomorrow's adventure for your meddling!"

It was a very good thing the kitten had insinuated itself when it did, Lord Waverly frowned to himself. A very good thing indeed. Selinda's eyes looked very large and her hair had begun to dry in soft ringlets about her face. If he had kissed her, he did not know where it might have ended. After all, there was no congregation to repress their passions this time, nor did he think, were any of the servants likely to enter without being summoned. Sternly pulling himself from Selinda's charms, Lord Waverly delivered her forthwith to Mrs. Fortnum's efficient care. As he retired to his own chamber, his imagination was full of visions of rapturous embraces, diminished only by the remonstrances of his conscience. Long into the night and early hours, he stared into the darkness waiting for sleep or morning—whichever came first.

Elsewhere on that dark and wretched night, Lucy and the rest of her party were as badly soaked as Selinda. In consequence of Prudence's having enjoined the driver to take them one village farther than had been planned in hopes of securing a room at less exorbitant cost, they had been caught in a powerful downpour. Almost immediately the wheels of their conveyance had become securely mired in several inches of sticky mud at a low spot in the road. While Rupert, Prudence, and the hapless coachman railed against their predicament and each other, Lucy stuck her head out the window and looked about. It was a desolate stretch of road.

It took several minutes before Prudence had exhausted her store of invectives and set her mind to deciding just what was to be done. Come what may, she was not about to spend the night in a damp coach.

"Well," she snapped poisonously at her son, "don't just sit there like a great slowtop. Get out and push."

"Wouldn't serve at all, Mater," he told her without budging. "If four horses cannot move the cursed thing, I hardly think my efforts would signify."

"Possibly not," his mother told him crushingly, "but the elimination of fifteen stone might."

More than usually sensitive about his weight since his horrifying nightmare, Rupert was in no mood to take this criticism without some sort of retaliation. "Perhaps," he spat, "you will join me outside the carriage, then, Mater. Where the loss of fifteen stone is a boon, will not thirty be a benediction?"

In the darkness there followed on this remark such a noise of grunts and slaps, that Lucy could only conjecture that one had set physically upon the other. Not at all wishing to have her own eyes blackened, she quietly opened the door and hopped forthwith out onto the lane where she stood in the rain, ankle deep in the dirt. By the flickering light of the lantern, she could see the coachman leaning up against the side of the vehicle, chewing his wad impassively as he trimmed his nails with a knife. Lucy watched in fascination as the rivulets ran down his face. Eventually, he spat into the darkness and regarded her with an indifferent expression.

"Nawt fer it but t'go back," he told her laconically. "Canna drive forward wi' that cursed load."

The carriage was still rattling from the combat within as Lucy returned his gaze. "How far back?" she asked finally, wiping a drip off the end of her nose.

"Oooh, mile or less, I'd say, from last inn. Looked right enough to me."

"What will you tell Aunt Prudence, Mr. . . . ?"

188

"Mugwort," he told her, spitting again. "Martin Mugwort. And I be tellin' that one nawt."

"Then whatever shall we do, Mr. Mugwort?" Lucy asked with some trepidation. "I should be glad to oblige and put in a word only I am not anxious to have my ears boxed. That is what always seems to happen when I open my mouth anymore. Anyway, I do not think I ought to go back inside the compartment until they have done with battering one another. And yet," she sighed with a little tremble, "it's cursed wet out here." At the end of this little speech, she looked appealingly at the coachman as she pulled the collar of her pelisse up about her chin.

At this, the grizzled Mugwort gave his shoulders a mighty shrug, but, as the skies opened with renewed intensity, he at last relented and beat vigorously at the side of the coach with his crop. "'Ere now!" he bellowed savagely into the midst of the brawl. "Enough o' that sorriness, devil take 'ee."

"Devil take yourself," was Rupert's eloquent reply. This remark, however, was quickly followed by a smart thwack in the darkness which apparently found its mark, for not another intelligible sound issued from the much-aggrieved fellow.

"Well, bumblewit," Prudence addressed the coachman as she thrust her head out the door, "what are you going to do, now that your cowhanded driving has got us in this mess?" Then spying Lucy, she aimed a cuff in that direction and, after accusing the child of being an artful, sneaking thing, commanded her to return to the carriage at once. In spite of the chilling downpour, Lucy hesitated a moment before complying.

Over the past several hours, Mugwort had contracted a violent antipathy for his principal passengers. The brat was right enough as brats went, but the others had used him scandalously every inch of the road to his way of thinking. He would never have driven out into this weather had he not been anticipating a generous tip from a group of what appeared at first to be gentry. Well, their speech had betrayed them immediately once their guard was down. He'd kept his ears open and knew well enough that terms such as that hideous jade had recently been casting at her son and himself did not fall from the lips of people of birth. He had a good mind to toss them out onto the mucky road and be done with them. At least without their burdensome weight, he had a fair idea his team could dislodge their load right enough.

Well, he resolved sagely, if there was to be any compensation for this night's hell, it seemed it must arise from seeing his passengers discommoded. Ignoring the last jibe, he opened the door all the way and announced, "Ye maun get out."

"Whatever do you mean, churl? Get out into the *wet?*" Prudence sputtered indignantly in his direction. "You belong in Bridewell!"

"It maun be," he told her implacably. "Wheels be buried up to God knows where wi' this damned load. Belike I got a pair o' millstones fer passengers."

190

It was this remark that catapulted Prudence into the roadway followed closely by her indignant son. It was one thing to exchange insults with relations, but to accept them from underlings such as this yokel was beyond bearing. As they slipped about in the mud, the coachman immediately scrambled back onto his perch with surprising agility and set about coaxing the horses forward. Indeed, he had been quite correct in his assessment of the situation. With Lucy as the only passenger, it was no trick at all for the team to extricate the mired coach and turn it back in the direction from which they had come.

"What idiotish trick is this, sapskull?" Prudence demanded belligerently, pounding on the side of the coach with the flat of her hand. "I mean for us to go forward tonight."

"Aye, then do," the coachman chortled unsympathetically. "For all that, I be goin' back. Ye be welcome to follow along by coach light, but that be all." With that, he gave the reins a quick shake and headed back in the direction of the last inn with the sounds of Rupert's and Prudence's abusive curses fading into the gale.

Inside the coach, Lucy was experiencing some mixed feelings as a result of this turn of events. She was glad she had obeyed Prudence's summons to return to the coach, and gratified, of course, to see her noxious guardians suffering vast discomfort. How diverting Lady Sybil must find all of this, she smiled to herself. It was then that the horrible thought struck her: Lady Sybil's ghost must have been left behind in the dark as well!

191

"What a horrid plaguey thing!" she cried aloud.

"What is that, child?" came a faint voice.

"Lady Sybil!" she cried with a sudden burst of happiness. "This is famous! But however do you come to be here? I thought you would be forced to stay with—"

"Well, yes, child . . . but just give me half a moment to recover." During the ensuing minutes, Lucy waited impatiently to hear the story. "There," the ghost finally said, "that will do nicely, I think. Well, how do I come to be here, you ask? I have just spent the last half-hour undoing the clasp on my necklace and extricating it from around that cow's thick neck. It fell to the floor during the scuffle, but it must still be in the coach or I would not be here. This really is a piece of luck, Lucy, for I vow she will assume she lost it in the mud! Now, all you have to do is find it and put it on, and I shall be able to follow you wherever you go."

With that, Lucy scrambled down onto the floor and, after a few minutes, sat back down bearing the lovely prize. In the dim light from the coach's lantern, the pearl and gold pomander glowed as richly as it did in Lady Sybil's portrait. Had she been capable, the ghost's eyes would have welled with tears at the sight of her favorite relation securing the lovely piece around her little neck. The thought of such a significant and much-loved item from her past buried in the folds of Prudence's wattled neck had incensed Lady Sybil no end. Here, she told herself as she looked at Lucy in the flickering light, was where it belonged.

"I feel so much better now, Lady Sybil," Lucy

told her in a voice edged with tears. "You cannot think how sad it was to watch you follow that creature about and leave me by myself. It was all I could do to keep my countenance . . . and my courage."

"I only hope we have time for a coze once we have arrived at the inn, for I believe we had better plan what to do when we get to Darrowdean. I do not trust that woman at all. She looks at you like a serpent eyeing a choice morsel, my dear."

"I hope, too," Lucy continued, suppressing a shudder, "that I can at least get into dry things before that ogress has me waiting on her, for I am sure that is what she will do. Oh, if only they would fall into the ditch and stay there. How odd! Now that I say the words, it seems to me I did dream of such a thing not long ago, so I expect it will come true. It was the same time I dreamed of you, although I hadn't a clue of who you were then. Just 'the lady who looks after us.' Oh, Lady Sybil, I do not know what I would have done without you!"

For the first time in her existence, the ghost knew the feeling of having been of service to another. It was, she thought to herself sentimentally, very nearly as good as an intrigue!

# Chapter Seventeen

Despite all odds, Lucy spent an unexpectedly pleasant night at a hospitable inn known as The Laughing Lion. Without further ado (but a fair amount of maliciousness), Mugwort had indeed driven on into the stormy night with a good deal more speed than he might have done, leaving Prudence and Rupert to trudge along through the rain and mud as best they could by the light of the ever-fading coach lamp. It was only two miles back to the inn, but for all Martin Mugwort cared, it might have been a league.

Within the dim compartment, Lucy shivered in her damp clothes. In spite of Lady Sybil's comforting prattle, she was still torn between enjoying her momentary relief and dreading the threat of imminent castigation. It had been a very trying day all the way around, and, in spite of her own woes, she could not help wondering how Selinda was faring with the vile Miss Snypish and whether Lord Waverly had yet spoken with her sister. She felt certain that the gentleman would be true to his word and watch her window for their agreed-upon distress signal, but she was worried that he might have driven by earlier that day, before events had compelled her to place the vase on the sill. Even if he had seen the yellow asters in her chamber window, how would he contrive to speak with Selinda and discover the details of her new difficulties? Lucy knew from sad experience that Miss Snypish was as tenacious a watchdog as any bull terrier, and, as the sounds of the storm whistled about the coach, she began to wonder if even the unparalleled Lord Waverly was equal to the tasks that lay ahead. In spite of his valiant efforts, so much might still go amiss. Lucy was overwrought indeed by the time the coach drew up to the welcoming lights of The Laughing Lion.

The inn was known far and near, not only for the excellence of its ale and bill of fare but for the warmth of its hospitality. At the first sight of the coach's tiny, forlorn passenger, Mrs. Bunche, the original proprietor's widow, gasped, clapped a hand to her heart, and gathered Lucy in from the throes of the tempest to the billowy comfort of her motherly breast.

"For the love o' God, Mart Mugwort," she exclaimed, "you'll be bringing me corpses next. Look at the white little face o' this one."

Instantly, the child found her cheeks pinched red, her wrists chafed raw, and her exhausted little self trundled off to bed with a hot posset before either she or the invisible Lady Sybil knew what was about. The chamber in which she was installed was one of the best, for there was little traffic on the road that night, and Mrs. Bunche hovered about directing chambermaids with bedwarmers and coal hods like a field marshal. When all was arranged to the good lady's satisfaction, she planted a noisy kiss on Lucy's forehead and wiped away a tear from her own cheek. "You've the look of my poor Alice before she was took," Mrs. Bunche sniffed. "Drink down your posset and go to sleep, child. And if any fret you 'fore morning, they shall have a sound thrashing from Mrs. Bessie Bunche!"

As the door quietly closed on the chamber, Lucy, with some difficulty, peered out over the tops of the three enormous feather ticks which had been piled over her.

"I have finally thought of what we must do, Lady Sybil," she whispered.

"Thank heaven," the ghost exclaimed. She had been taxing her poor resources for some time now, but had come up with nothing.

"I think the best thing is to send Lord Waverly a note to say what has happened. I still have the gold sovereigns he gave me," she continued meditatively. "Surely that is enough to send a message quickly and quietly."

Considering the sort of service such a sum would have purchased in her day, Lady Sybil assured Lucy that these funds would surely be sufficient. At that, the child crawled from under the covers, made her way to the door, and peeked out into the corridor. Several servants were bustling about, but Lucy waited until she spied a

196

lad with a wide, honest face who appeared to be only a few years older than herself. Briefly, she made arrangements to have some writing materials brought and a message sent, displaying just one of the gold pieces as evidence of her wherewithal. In only a few moments, Lucy faced pen, ink, paper, and sealing wax assembled before her on a table. Outside in the corridor, her youthful messenger waited with visions of an unprecedented journey to the capital dancing in his head and a promise of confidentality sealing his lips.

"Do you think," Lady Sybil ventured as the child concentrated on her task, "that it might not be wise to inform someone else of your predicament? Times may have changed, but I imagine letters still go astray."

"You are right, of course, Lady Sybil," Lucy admitted, knitting her brow in consternation, "but I cannot imagine who . . . unless . . ."

"Yes?" the ghost prompted.

"I wonder if I might not send a message to Lord Waverly's man of business."

"He must already have left for the country, more's the pity," the ghost sighed.

"But I know his direction," Lucy smiled suddenly. "Mr. Noon is staying at The Golden Hour."

Below in the taproom, before a roaring fire, Mrs. Bunche turned her attention to Martin Mugwort who was availing himself of her best brew. In spite of her comforting gestures of a few moments earlier, the good lady's suspicions had been much aroused, and, when she finally sat herself down across from the coachman, she fixed him with a gaze of penetrating scrutiny.

"Well, it will be a wonder if that poor child doesn't take an ague and die of it this very evening," was her optimistic assessment. "Howsomever, that's not the half of it, I'll warrant. Unless I miss my mark, there's something not quite on the up and up here. I know well enough from the set of her shoulders she's gentry, but how does a child of that age come to be traveling in a hired coach all by herself, I ask you? I couldn't turn her away and call myself Christian, but I'll be bound there'll be trouble of it! Now tell me what I need to know, Mugwort, and don't try to wriggle yourself out of it."

The coachman regarded this formidable adversary through narrowed eyes as he considered what to tell her. His animosity toward Prudence and Rupert had not abated one whit but had instead intensified more and more with each pint of ale he put down.

"Poor little mite," he told her at last, shaking his grizzled head. "Bein' sent away to work at a mill by a pair of crool relations."

At this revelation, Mrs. Bunche drew in her breath sharply and threw her hands up to her ample face. "That wisp of a child to work in one of them criminal mills? Bless us and save us all! And she was sent to meet that fate all by herself?"

"Oh, they sent an abigail, right and tight enow, nasty spidery thing she was, too. But midnight last she took fit and died. 'Orrible sight it were,"

Mugwort told her with an eloquent leer. "'Er eyes popped out 'n' spun like tops. It were a picture. But dinna fret yoursel', missus. You'll not be put out for long. I sent word this noon and the brat's aunt and cousin be coming themselves to fetch her to the mill. Won't be any trouble once they be here. Should be soon, too, I don't wonder. Y'know, the mills be desperate fond o' the little 'uns. They send 'em into the works to fetch out rats as 've got squashed there. Nothin' like a great fat rat to spoil a bolt o' cloth." Happy with this fabrication, he took another long quaff of ale.

"Devils!" the lady pronounced with a dark expression. "Take that angel child to certain death, will they? Not if Bessie Bunche has aught to say about it!"

"That's as may be, but I dinna know how the likes of you could stop 'em, missus. They be a great fat pair. Mean as mustard, too."

Good Mrs. Bunche considered the matter for about as long as it took the inventive coachman to swallow down the last of his ale. "Mean they may be," she told him with a stalwart glint, "but they've met their match in Bessie Bunche, I'll be bound. Just you watch, Mart Mugwort, and I'll show you how I serve the likes of them knaves."

Mrs. Bunche had no sooner spoken these words than the soaking figures of Rupert and his mother at last staggered into the inn's front hallway.

"Fetch us a noggin of rum and be quick about it, woman," Prudence commenced as she flung her wet wrap onto the floor. "And tell that sniveling brat, wherever she's cowering, to make herself useful. I suppose she's stuffing her face here at our expense."

Surreptitiously, the coachman watched with no small amusement as a dangerously livid shade rose in Mrs. Bunche's round face. Without preamble, she pulled a poker from the rack near the fireplace and waved it menacingly at the dripping pair before her.

"Out!" she commanded in a steely tone. "We've no room nor patience either for your likes. Fiends from hell the both of you!"

Prudence, whose face had likewise become quite crimson with anger, opened her mouth, but the crude retort she had formulated stuck in her throat. Rupert, who had never before seen his mother speechless, could but stare at such a wonder.

"Out!" Mrs. Bunche continued, her anger rising. "Out, or I'll set the dogs on you! Don't think I don't know all about your criminal connivance! There's something not right here or my name's not Bessie Bunche. What's more, I have an idea what it is. Lay a hand to that child, and I'll call the magistrate. I think he might be very interested in the cruel intentions of certain family members—if that's what you've the boldness to call yourselves."

Neither the coachman nor Mrs. Bunche had any idea of the extent to which her accusations were being misinterpreted by the guilty pair, but Prudence's scarlet face quickly became ashen and Rupert's eyes widened to the point of pain. Without another word they began to back once more toward the door.

"Aye, that's the way to go," Mrs. Bunche continued, still holding the poker ominously. "You can spend the night in the barn if the cattle don't mind, but I'll not have the likes of you under this honest roof. Now just you keep going the way you came."

Although the rain continued to fall unabated, driven on by the rising wind, Prudence and Rupert, in silent unison, chose to brave its ferocity. As soon as they had exited, Mrs. Bunche nodded to herself with grim satisfaction, set the poker back in its rack, and wiped her hands on her apron. Her duty as protector of the helpless discharged, however, she once again shouldered the office of innkeeper and, seemingly oblivious to the inconsistency of her actions, immediately set about ordering several servants to carry dinner, blankets, feather ticks, and hot water out to the barn. "Let it never be said," she told the coachman with a toss of her head, "that any received scant hospitality at The Laughing Lion."

This oddly sorted cordiality was met with little grace by her two guests even though they devoured every morsel and snarled over who should have the better of the blankets. Munching on a huge wedge of cheddar, Prudence cast an appraising eye over the cattle in the barn. Several of the horses looked as if they might carry her weight. It had been a number of years since she had ridden, but she thought she might still be equal to such an activity. A horse would take her to Darrowdean faster than a coach anyway, and, if the insinuations the wretched woman in the inn had cast at her meant that even an iota of the truth about her plotting was known, time was of the essence. The brat had best be deserted. A pity, she thought, for her plans for vengeance had begun to amuse her, but there was nothing else for it.

Even so, it disturbed Prudence to think that she had become so overwrought that she backed down in the face of adversity. Ordinarily, she would have faced the accusations with aplomb. Now that she was out of the storm and off her tired feet, she realized that the woman could not possibly have known anything. That wretched Lucy must, of course, have told some sort of vile falsehood, for Prudence was sure the brat, too, was largely ignorant of the truth of her situation.

Old age. That was it. The long day's travel and the horrid trek through the detestable mud and wet had undone her entirely. She must be losing her edge, Prudence thought sadly, and her vision of a tropical escape never seemed so appealing. In the dim lantern light, she shrugged off her wet gown and huddled miserably into a pile of blankets. A few moments of warmth would surely restore her, she decided sleepily. Rupert was already snoring loudly, and, to the accompaniment of his sonorous droning, her eyes grew heavier and heavier.

When at last Prudence's head rested on her chest and her own resonant sawing filled the air, Rupert's wheezing suddenly abated. It had served his purposes more than once during his youth to feign slumber until his mother had dropped off to sleep, and tonight was no exception. The day's misadventure, following so quickly on the sad erosion of his relationship with his mother, had further convinced him that all ties to her must be severed without further ado. He had noticed during the day that her gown sagged in a most peculiar manner, and he suspected that she had sewn a good deal of the fortune she had amassed thus far into its generous seams. When she had undressed a few moments earlier, the garment had fallen to the ground with a resounding slap for which its wet fabric alone could not be accountable.

He would wait an hour or so until she had entered a deep sleep, he decided. But as soon as he deemed it safe, he would take possession of the dress and its precious contents and make his own way to Darrowdean. He could transact the sale just as well as his mother should he choose to follow that course of action; on the other hand, however, it might better serve his purposes to maintain the property. He still cherished fond hopes of wiggling himself into Selinda's good graces. Perhaps his preservation of her childhood home would earn him some gratitude; and if, in the course of things, his mother were mistaken for a derelict and sent off to a workhouse or asylum, so much the better.


When Lord Waverly found himself greeting the pinkish hues of sunrise for the second time in a mere week, he assured himself with an enormous yawn that this must indeed be love. Pulling himself from the feathery depths of his bed, he quickly set about preparing for what he feared would be an arduous day. Lady Selinda had made it quite plain on the previous night that she would not be gainsayed in her desire to make up one half of the rescue party, in spite of the physical and emotional distress she had suffered on the previous evening.

Though the autumn morning was clear, Lord Waverly's thoughts were still as confused as they had been when he finally drifted into sleep. He could think of no more pleasant pastime than traveling through the golden countryside with the woman he loved; however, the *other* question still loomed: should he allow Selinda to expose herself to compromise and censure? He frowned into the glass as he tied his cravat, recalling Selinda's threat to follow after him regardless. His experience with her was limited, of course, but, if Lucy's description of her older sister's fearlessness was accurate, he suspected that the lady was entirely capable of making good on her promise. There was always the possibility, he reminded himself, that, after the thorough soaking to which she had been subjected last night, Selinda might think better of her wish to accompany him and keep to her bed. Early mornings, after all, often prompted such decisions. Yes, of course, he thought grimly. And the Prince Regent might very likely enter a monastery as well.

Thus, on making his way down the stairs, Lord Waverly was not terribly surprised to find that the object of his meditations had preceded him to the breakfast parlor where she was acquitting herself quite admirably. He was, of course, much gratified to confirm that she had not, as so many others might have done, gone off into an immediate decline. In fact, she was almost rosy with anticipation of the day's events and most certainly restored to looks. Her dress and cloak had been set to rights, and, by way of toilette, she had tied back her tumbled locks with one of his cravats. She looked determinedly charming and, clearly, ready for anything.

"Good morning, Lord Waverly," she began briskly as she poured him a cup of coffee. "How long do you think until we set out?"

Selinda looked up at him with a smile, and suddenly Lord Waverly's spirits lightened. To see her seated at his own table, looking so very much as if that were her proper sphere, made him smile in turn and swallow his fears and misgivings. All would be well, he assured himself.

"I hope it shall not be long," Selinda went on quickly without waiting for his reply, "for you must own it would never do if Miss Snypish were to discover my absence and set someone after me."

Lord Waverly agreed that this was so and informed her of his decision to have his landau sent around. Although he did not see fit to mention it, comfort was not Lord Waverly's primary concern in his choice of conveyance. He was by nature so little used to thinking about propriety that Richard's insinuations about Selinda's character last night, however mistaken, had taken Lord Waverly aback. Although his anger had resulted in the servant's dismissal, his nocturnal deliberations had prompted him to choose a closed vehicle for the journey. Selinda would be conveyed in comfort and anonymity. He himself would ride ahead to gather what information he might and, he realized as he looked across the table at her, wisely avoid the temptation a day's companionship might inspire.

"The rain subsided during the night," he told her with a smile, "and I think we shall get along quickly enough—more so, to be sure, than the heavily laden coach we pursue. They will have had a hard night of it. I do not think they can be far ahead of us."

At this speech, Selinda's smile broadened prettily, for she had been steeped in a very real fear that she would not be allowed to go after all. She had been entirely serious in her threat to follow, but, in her heart, she knew well enough she had not the least clue as to how to set about it. Certainly, she had read about intrepid heroines who had undergone any number of hardships in pursuit of honor and heart's desire, but whether *she* was equal to such bold actions—that was another question. Apparently, though, Lord Waverly believed her to be a more capable sort than she did herself. That was heartening anyway. Relieved, however, that she would not be forced to discover the true extent of her resourses, she contentedly finished her breakfast.

Before another half-hour had passed and indeed before the last tinges of pink had disappeared from the horizon, Lord Waverly's traveling coach was departing London.

# Chapter Eighteen

Selinda need not have worried that the discovery of her absence was at all imminent. When Miss Snypish finally arose from her bed the next day, the morning was all but spent and the sun high in the sky. It had rained hard during the night, of course, but now the air was brisk and clear. A new day and a new life beckoned to the companion. Miss Snypish threw open the window and her thin lips hovered momentarily on the edge of a smile. It felt rather odd, she decided, but not unpleasant.

She was excited about the expedition to Madame Tussaud's Waxworks, of course, but even more so by the thought of the Marquess of Bastion's attendance on her. He really was perfect, she sighed inwardly. He bowed and complimented and fawned very nicely, but, best of all, he listened to what she said and repeated it back to her as veriest wisdom. Her heart beat with a newborn passion.

As she settled herself in front of her glass, Miss

Snypish examined her face with satisfaction. It certainly did appear that the last few days' treatments and her change in diet had been efficacious. She thought she could see the beginnings of color in her sallow cheeks and even, perhaps, a bit of a glow. She would wear the cerise crepe that had been delivered late yesterday and perhaps the round bonnet with the turquoise bows. Yes, the ribbon would set it all off nicely, she thought. Then she remembered the yellow roses the marquess had sent the day before. Perhaps she would do him the honor of pinning some of them to the crown of the bonnet. A less determined woman might have eschewed such a ploy, but she did not balk in the least at emotional manipulation.

There was just one other thing, though. Selinda. The older woman frowned as she envisioned the girl's delicate features. Perhaps her tale of Selinda's failing health was insufficient. Even though Miss Snypish was fairly certain that the marquess had believed her fabrication of the day before, she was not at all certain she wanted any sort of rival about. Perhaps it would serve well to have Selinda keep to her chamber today. After all, the girl had looked quite faded the day before and even at dinner last night. A day or two of seclusion could do her no harm. Then Miss Snypish could have both Bastion and his cousin to herself. It would not do the marquess a bit of harm to suspect that he might have a rival for her affections. And, after all, her employers would return all too soon, and Miss Snypish wanted to secure her position with her suitor as quickly as possible.

Suddenly determined, she pulled a faded wrapper about her lean form and strode down the hallway to Selinda's chamber. Without the formality of a knock, she threw open the door and made her way across the darkened room to the window. It was high time the girl was up and about, she tut-tutted to herself. It really was not like Selinda to sleep away half the day. She flung the curtains wide, and, turning to pounce on her slumbering victim, she stopped in her tracks. Selinda's bed was empty and undisturbed.

In another part of the city, Richard, Lord Waverly's former footman, sat glowering at nothing in particular. His erstwhile master and that troublemaking miss had departed almost before it was light, leaving instructions for the servant to be gone before the day was out. The clock in the drawing room had just rung two. Richard had completed packing his belongings and now sat in the elegant foyer one last time, delaying the inevitable moment when he must leave. It seemed a sad and sorry miscarriage of justice, he reflected bitterly, that, just because he had conducted affairs according to his superior notion of what was proper, an exemplary servant should have received not only such a blistering tongue-lashing but an unprecedented dismissal. After all, it was not as if his Lordship had prepared him for what was to happen last night. How was he to know that an errand to convey a message would transform to one of delivering a miss? Well, he had done his best to be circumspect and it had got him nowhere.

Richard's frown deepened. Times were hard and it would be next to impossible to find another position as profitable. True, his Lordship's odd ways had rankled and chafed, but the wages he paid were unparalleled. Richard had momentarily considered what he might do to find his way back into Waverly's good graces, but, as he recalled his employer's parting words, he knew that sort of turnaround was not to be looked for. He must begin to search out a position where his talents would be appreciated, and straightaway, too.

Just then, the front doorbell sounded. Richard straightened himself with habitual precision and opened the door. Before him stood a young boy, certainly no more than twelve or thirteen, covered in mud and gnawing on an apple. An expression of severe disdain for this extraordinary effrontery appeared on Richard's face, and he immediately made as if to shut the door against this most distressing sight.

"'Ere now, not so fast, mister," the boy cried out, quickly slipping past the repressive Richard. "I got a message for 'is Lordship and it's urgent pressing."

Richard, quite naturally, had been about to toss the boy back onto the street and would have done so had he been able to determine how to accomplish that feat without actually having to touch the creature. Even though his loathing for Lord Waverly had reached a fevered pitch, the sight of the urchin's bare feet on the mirrorlike

210

marble prompted in Richard a severe and sudden nausea.

"It's from a lady," the boy added in a whisper.

"From a lady, you say?" Richard gasped, firmly repressing his stomach's rebellion.

"A very young lady, if you take my meaning."

Richard pursed his lips and thought for a moment. Distressing though the messenger was, the envelope he clutched in his grubby hand was intriguing. Whatever it was, it might bear some fruit if Richard could contrive to use it to his advantage.

"I shall take it to his Lordship as soon as he has arisen," Richard intoned loftily. "Now take a farthing and run along."

The boy hesitated a moment. He had promised the little girl at the inn that he would personally see the message put into Lord Waverly's hands. Still, he thought, there was no telling how long the gentleman would sleep, and he was planning on spending the day looking about the city. He had been paid generously to deliver the message, but what good was that if he was forced to spend the day cooling his heels instead of enjoying the sights? It couldn't hurt, he reasoned, to entrust the message to a servant who looked, to his provincial eyes, like a veritable member of the nobility himself.

"You'll be sure 'e gets it?" the boy asked with a suspicious glare.

By way of reply, Richard raised one very daunting eyebrow and motioned the boy toward the door. Shrugging, the messenger turned and took himself down the street in search of amusement.

Once he was alone, Richard wasted no time in acquainting himself with the contents of the message. It was inexpertly sealed, and, heating the edge of a gilt letter opener in a candle, he was quickly able to slide the blade beneath the wax without disturbing the impression. There, in large, round handwriting he read:

*My dear Lord Waverly,*

*We are in a sorry state, indeed, for I have been forced to go along with my wretched guardians whom you know I have cause to fear. We are at an inn called The Laughing Lion, or at least I am, for my tormentors have luckily been lost in the storm—may they never find their road! That is all foolishness and wishful thinking, though, for anyone can see they will make their way here soon enough.*

*Selinda is all alone at Harroweby House, but for that vile Miss Snypish who you will agree is as evil as ink. I do not know what else to tell you, but, if it is not too terribly inconvenient, could you perhaps rescue me? I do not like to own it, but I begin to be very much afraid.*

*If everything should fall out badly, I must thank you now for all your efforts. But do hurry, for I am being as brave as I can. You will look after Selinda, I know, for you love her.*

*Lady Lucy Harroweby*

Harroweby, Richard smiled to himself. Fortune favors those who keep their eyes open to the main chance, he reminded himself. Well, he would just gather up his bags and hie himself to Harroweby House. Doubtless someone there would be very interested in the contents of this letter. And doubtless, he reflected with a thin smile, they would feel some gratitude toward him.

Selinda sat inside Lord Waverly's coach watching the countryside slide swiftly by. The last time she had driven along this road, her circumstances had been different but no less harrowing. Why was it, she wondered, that such adventures seemed so much more agreeable on the printed page than in real life? Her situation entailed all of the classic components of love and adventure stories, but only in dreams had she achieved the effects of which she had read. As Selinda recalled her shocking dream of two nights ago, she realized that it no longer brought a blush to her cheeks, only a mysterious warmth that transcended the hardships that surrounded her.

But still, she reminded herself harshly, a dream was merely a dream. True, Lord Waverly had kissed her during their extraordinary encounter under the church pew and held her most comfortingly in the park. And then again he was about to kiss her last night until that pesky cat had insinuated itself between them. But what was there in that? Everything except a declaration of love, she thought ruefully. It was clear that Lord

Waverly was a brave and generous man who cared not one whit for the opinion of society, but, very likely, it was her remarkable little sister who had charmed him and not her more conventional self. Selinda looked sadly down at the woolen gown she wore and the heavy shoes she had donned in preparation for her damp vigil of the previous night. In spite of her troubles, she no more resembled a romantic heroine than Miss Snypish did. Well, she grinned ruefully, perhaps a *little* more romantic than that person, but not as much as she would like to imagine.

In confirmation of these dreary meditations, Selinda had seen but little of Lord Waverly since their journey began. He had for the greater part of the day ridden on ahead, in hopes, he had told her, of hearing something of the coach in which Lucy had departed with Prudence and Rupert. As mile after mile spun by, Selinda began to feel like one more piece of baggage rather than an equal partner in Lucy's rescue. More than anything, she wished for a happy conclusion to this distressing tale, but it would be splendid indeed if she could be a part of bringing it about rather than a mere observer. Selinda was about to give herself over to despondency when she remembered that Lord Waverly had, at last, returned her book to her. What good fortune! However little the events in her life were mirrored therein, she could at least pretend.

# Chapter Nineteen

Miss Snypish flew about her chamber, desperately arranging her toilette. The sight of Selinda's empty bed had brought her heart to her throat and the image of Prudence's wrathful expression to her mind's terrified eye. She was not at all clear what she must do in order to recover the wretched girl, but, whatever it was, she was at least sensible to the fact that she could not accomplish it dressed only in her wrapper.

The distraught companion made herself decent in record time, tore down the staircase and out the front door where she ran bodily into a footman bearing a note. As he picked himself up off the walk, she could not help noticing that his livery identified him as belonging to Lord Waverly's house.

In spite of her normally staid demeanor, Miss Snypish was so relieved by the appearance of one unconnected with Harroweby House (and thus unlikely to inform her employers of her charge's disappearance) who might possibly be able to assist her in her sudden need that she was unable to restrain the shrill whoop of elation that rose to her lips. Taking the startled Richard (for indeed it was he) firmly by the ear, she dragged him back the way she had come, slammed the door after her, and sat her victim down in a hooded chair. There she stood before him, effectively blocking any path of escape, her eyes glittering with ominous desperation.

"Well?" she demanded at last, holding her hand out for the note.

Richard, with such courage as would have astonished his most recent employer, cleared his throat and, holding aside the message he had intercepted, begged leave to have some speech with the master or mistress of the house. This request Miss Snypish ignored with a disdainful snort, and, kicking the poor fellow soundly in the shin, she caused him to let go his prize as he gasped and clutched both hands to his now-throbbing leg. The companion, who during the early days of her current post had been assigned the duties of governess as well, at once recognized Lucy's round hand as the letter fluttered to the ground. With a gasp, she snatched it up and, with neither permission nor ceremony, immediately began to peruse it.

Through his pain, Richard watched with fascination as the woman's face grew quite gray beneath her paint. "Do you know the direction of the Marquess of Bastion?" she managed at last.

"Naturally," Richard sneered. "The marquess is the first cousin of—"

"Then you shall come with me," she informed him, fixing him with an icy stare which made his knees suddenly weak with trepidation. "Come, sirrah. We shall summon a hackney at once."

Half an hour later, the Marquess of Bastion's similarly intimidated valet was hastily assisting his master in a rushed toilette. From the servant's stuttering description, Bastion had no doubt that his caller was the inestimable Miss Snypish, but he had not the least idea what had prompted her to make such an untoward call. If nothing else, however, he had come to value that woman's good sense so like his own, and decided that she must have an unusually good motive.

When at last he joined her in his parlor, he was exceedingly surprised to see her accompanied by Richard, his cousin's footman. What in the devil was going on here? he wondered. Before he could inquire, however, Miss Snypish wordlessly handed him Lucy's note. When he at last looked up at her, she managed to say with tight control, "As you can see, my lord, we have been scandalously used."

It was unfortunate that the marquess was not so swift a thinker as she and it was several moments before the situation as she had deduced it, confirmed halfheartedly by the terrified Richard, could be explained to his satisfaction. When the import of the message at last struck him, Bastion was torn between a smug elation in learning that his cousin had done something so despicable as to elope with a defenseless heiress and anger that his own similar plans had been thwarted.

"I think I shall have a brandy," he said at last.

"I think you shall do no such thing," Miss Snypish told him sharply. "We must pursue them at once!"

The marquess frowned. "Pursue them in what? I have a high-perch phaeton, but—"

"Then, sir, a high-perch phaeton it must be," Miss Snypish cut him off, "for I shall not have the fortunes of some blighted while others prosper with impunity. Now let us be off."

"So you mean us to head for this Laughing Lion?" the marquess ventured.

Miss Snypish sighed heavily and swallowed the crushing epithet that rose so easily to her lips. In fact, had not the weakness of his chin prompted such tender ardor in her bosom, she might well have boxed his ears. "No, no," she said evenly at last. "Lord Waverly and Lady Selinda know nothing of The Laughing Lion, do they? *We* have Lucy's little note, after all. We shall, of *course*, head for Darrowdean and intercept the pair."

"And then?" the marquess persisted blankly.

"I shall tell you when we get there," Miss Snypish returned, sinking inwardly as she realized she had not the least idea.

Lucy awoke to a brilliant blue day after a night of singularly pleasant dreams. Indeed, her nocturnal visions of ices at Gunter's and entertainments at Astley's Amphitheatre were so peopled with handsome young boys that she was forced to look at the spirit of her frolicsome great-great grandmama quite narrowly. She would have taxed the ghost with her rising suspicions had not Mrs. Bunche just then entered the chamber singing a country song in cheerful inaccurate tones.

"So you survived the night, my poor little dove," Mrs. Bunche crooned. "And how are we feeling, pet?"

"Quite well, thank you," Lucy told her, smiling her crooked smile. "Whatever time is it? I feel it must be quite sinfully late."

"It is well past midday, but never mind the time, sweeting. Just tell me true—can it be you've no grippe? No ague? No putrification of the lung?"

"Indeed, I do not think so!" the child exclaimed, her eyes wide.

Unconvinced, Mrs. Bunche felt Lucy's forehead and, pronouncing it to be as cool as a root cellar wall, commenced to worry that Lucy had been chilled so thoroughly as to defy the ability to take a fever. It took some minutes for Lucy to persuade the good soul that she felt extremely tolerable.

Still, Mrs. Bunche frowned at her and exclaimed that she could not like the worry line that was beginning to form between the child's eyes.

"Not that I blame you, my turtle dove, for—I vow!—to be tormented with the likes of those two devilish fiends as followed you here last night would set a corn-fed sow to worriting itself."

At the mention of this pair, Lucy did indeed begin to fret herself, particularly when the proprietress informed her of the lodgings her supposed relations had suffered during the night. This revelation conjured up such a comical picture, however, that Lucy did indulge in a brief laugh, especially as she was able to see Lady Sybil convulse in mirth and throw her spectral arms around Mrs. Bunche's neck. Lucy soon recovered herself, however. "To be sure, they deserve no better, for they are the most shocking creatures imaginable, Mrs. Bunche," Lucy confided with a little tremble. "I cannot but dread that such a reception will only make them behave worse toward me than they have already done."

"Have no fear of that, my sweeting," the good lady said, tweaking her under the chin rather painfully. "The groom awoke this morning to find two of my horses gone, and I have sent the magistrate and his deputies after them. You may rest your head and drink your chocolate in peace, lovey, if that sorry snail of a kitchen maid will but bring it up. What's more, if no decent soul claims you for kin, I shall keep you myself!"

Lucy was just raising her eyebrows at this thought when the door was opened by a slight chambermaid bearing a tray so heavily laden with victuals that she proceeded into the room slightly alist.

"So there you are at last, Mopsa," Mrs. Bunche grumbled in exasperated tones. "I do not know when I have seen such a sorry slowcoach!"

The said Mopsa teetered precariously toward the fireside table and set down her burden with a resounding thud before answering her mistress. "But Mrs. Bunche," she squeaked excitedly, bobbing a hasty curtsey, "there is such news! I'm sure you must forgive me when I tell you, for there is the hugest uproar down t'village as ever I saw, no nor me mum neither."

"What?" Mrs. Bunche snorted disdainfully. "Have the tinkers passed through town again?"

"No, nor Gypsies either, though I dearly love a Gypsy!" the girl burbled with excitement. "And you will recall, I know, that black-eyed devil who would have carried me off to have his foul way with me, but that I told him I'd never have him. Yes, Gypsies—"

"Enough of Gypsies, girl," Mrs. Bunche cried. "I vow you will drive me cockeyed with your nonsense! Now what is this uproar you speak of?"

"Uproar! You do well to call it so, Mrs. Bunche! You will not credit it, but there's two foul criminals locked in the stocks, and they are using such sorry language as would make the devil himself blush."

"Is that all, ninny?" the older woman scolded. "Why, those stocks haven't a moment to grow cool between victims, we live in such sorry times. Now, Mopsa, you go right now and—"

"Oh, but that ain't the half of it, Mrs. Bunche," the girl continued breathlessly, fanning herself with the bottom of her apron, "for one were a great fat lady and she riding a horse through town chasing hot as you please after a fat man . . ."

"My horses!" Mrs. Bunche exclaimed.

". . . who was yelping like anything for she kept smacking at him with a crop . . ."

"Great heavens!" Lucy chimed in.

". . . and she were all but mother-naked for he had stolen her gown . . ."

"Lord-a-mercy!" Mrs. Bunche cried.

221

". . . and soon enough she smacked his horse and it reared and whinnied so that it frightened *her* horse who reared, too, and straightaway didn't they both end face down, arse up in a mucky ditch . . ."

"Hoorah!" shouted Lucy.

". . . where the magistrate found them slinging mud and curses and—bless him—had them both clapped in irons and taken to the stocks! What's more, they shall be locked in the gaol at sundown."

At the end of this remarkable speech, Mopsa curtseyed once again and began laying out Lucy's nuncheon as if nothing untoward had happened at all. Mrs. Bunche, not one to miss out on excitement of this order, exited the chamber immediately, and soon enough Lucy could hear her calling loudly for her gig to be harnessed. When Mopsa had completed her task and bobbed her way out, Lucy sprang from the bed, pulled off the huge nightrail with which Mrs. Bunche had supplied her on the previous night and began to dress herself.

"Whatever do you make of this business, Lady Sybil?" she asked as she wiggled into her chemise.

The ghost, who had been peering out the window to see if the village were at all visible from their vantage point, turned and smiled triumphantly. "I believe that fate has at last taken a hand in your difficulties, Lucy. I trust you may now sit quiet until Lord Waverly or his agent arrives, for I am sure it will be sometime today."

Lucy frowned and fingered the gold pomander she wore around her neck. By daylight it was clear that it had received a fair battering on the floor of the coach the night before, for several of the pearls were missing and the catch was bent. At least, however, it had not lost the facility of keeping Lady Sybil by her side. Sitting quietly and waiting for events to shape themselves was not at all what she had been used to lately. But in spite of her reassurances to Mrs. Bunche, she had to admit that she did feel somewhat fagged, even after a good night's sleep. Perhaps a quiet day was in order, after all. Yawning, she crossed to the window and stood beside the ghost. The sun was now well past its summit and the inn yard was quite busy. Boys ran after chicken, two mud-specked horses were being led toward the barn even as Mrs. Bunche in her gig drove out, and milkmaids chatted companionably in the shade of a golden oak. In the distance, Lucy could see a vehicle approaching the inn accompanied by an outrider. There was something about the party that attracted Lucy's attention, and suddenly she felt a strange buzz course through her. Even though the vehicle and rider were little more than dots on the horizon, she knew with an uncanny uncertainty that Lord Waverly had come at last.

*. . . Rosamonde at last looked into the depths of Roderick's eyes,* Selinda was reading, *and recognized in them a mirror of her own overriding love and passion. The sun was just rising over the misty reaches of Larksdown Moor, and the song of the waking birds echoed at last in her heart.*

*"The depths of our love cannot be sounded,"* Roderick whispered in awed tones, *"nor the brilliance of our devotion sullied. Say you will be my wife . . ."*

"How can you doubt me?" Selinda murmured, caught up in her fantasy world.

"Lady Selinda?" came Lord Waverly's voice.

She looked up with a blushing start. Her book, now that she had it back, had so stolen the focus from her worries that she had not even realized that the coach had come to a stop. Surely, she told herself, she could not have spoken aloud!

"We shall be changing horses at this inn," Lord Waverly was saying. "The Laughing Lion, it is called. I think you must wish to refresh yourself. I shall bespeak a private parlor, of course, but . . ."

"Yes?"

"There is," he went on hesitantly, "the matter of the proprietor's customary curiosity. I own I had forgotten that small matter, but my driver has reminded me that it is always so. You would not mind if I identified you as my wife?"

Selinda sighed. How similar, yet how different from the declaration she had just read in her little book. "Of course. I am sure that is most wise," was all she said, however. What a fool she was to allow herself to dream.

Lord Waverly escorted her into the inn bearing a heavy heart. He had hoped a little wildly that she might honor his suggestion with at least a smile of encouragement, but she had only sighed. What had he expected? Even she must know that, for all his wealth, his connections, and, yes, his thoroughly engaged heart, he was considered an odd case by all and sundry. True, she had returned his kiss in the church—well, he *had* surprised her—and allowed herself to be comforted in the park when she felt herself to be assailed at all sides. And last night? Something had perhaps *almost* happened, but what of it? It was clear she knew no more of the world than that little orange kitten. He, who should have known better, ought not to read more into her smiles and veiled glances than was there. Life, after all, was not a book.

Since Mrs. Bunche had left in a flurry some few minutes before their arrival, Lord Waverly and Lady Selinda stood in the entry of The Laughing Lion waiting for someone to notice their arrival. Each was occupied with his or her own gloomy thoughts and concerns, the corners of their mouths turned decidedly down, and each started with surprise when they heard a familiar voice from above cry out, "It *is* you! Famous!"

# Chapter Twenty

The Marquess of Bastion was thoroughly lost. Even though it was Miss Snypish who held the map and she who had given directions, he did not feel at all equal to telling her that this countryside looked nothing like any corner of England he had ever visited on purpose. They had, he recalled now, taken a number of odd turns. It seemed to him that they were traveling south along the road rather than due north as they should have been. He had for most of the morning been rather preoccupied with the oddity he was sure they must present to all observers: a smart perch phaeton with dashing yellow wheels all besmirched with dirt and peopled by a desperate-looking couple. He hoped that no one mistook them for a pair of elopers. Of course, he reminded himself, if they were heading south, no one must think that.

The marquess sighed and stole a glance at his companion. She did not seem disconcerted in the least. He could not have explained to anyone—

certainly not his friend, the Earl of Slaverington—the creeping fascination he felt stealing over him like a rash. As he looked at Miss Snypish's resolute profile, something in him stirred profoundly.

"Turn right at the crossroads," the lady directed him.

"Maidstone?" he inquired blankly, looking at the sign. "What? Are we in Kent, then?"

Miss Snypish nodded and commanded him to drive on. They had indeed turned south earlier in the day and executed a number of circuitous turns, but she had been relying on the marquess's ignorance—which seemed to be vast—and a natural want of curiosity to prevent his questioning her on the route she had elected.

She and the marquess had begun their journey full of rancor and dire vows of vengeance, but it had presently occurred to Miss Snypish that, while vengeance was sweet, it could profit her not at all. As the day progressed, she had guided the marquess farther and farther away from their quarry and deeper into territory she knew quite well: the rambling countryside of Kent.

It was only a short distance from the crossroads to Maidstone. A short distance, too, she hoped, from the drudgery of her life as a poor spinster companion to the splendor of becoming the Marchioness of Bastion. As they drove into the center of the town, Miss Snypish requested that the marquess pull up in front of a respectable-looking house. Taking his whip from him she leaned out over the edge of the phaeton and snapped it resolutely against what appeared to be a parlor window. It was not long before a homely woman in a mobcap appeared in the doorway. A look of unmitigated terror appeared on the servant's face. Her mouth opened into a small o, and she gasped in a low tone, "The Stone Maid of Maidstone!"

"What's that she says?" the marquess inquired, turning a little pale.

"Where is the magistrate, Lizzie?" Miss Snypish demanded quickly, ignoring his question. "Summon him at once!"

Reacting immediately to this strident command, the woman bobbed and scurried back into the house. In just a few moments a sour-faced man appeared in the midst of polishing his spectacles. When at last he adjusted them on the end of his long, pointy nose, he gasped, "Letitia! Can that be you? What the devil brings you back to Maidstone?"

"Yes, Papa, it is I," she returned grimly. "This gentleman"—and here she tapped the marquess with the whip she still held—"has abducted me."

Bastion, the dawn of understanding rising at last in his eyes, turned and stared at her with a mixture of terror and admiration.


Lucy scurried down the stairs and threw her arms first around Selinda and then Lord Waverly. Although she had maintained a brave front for the past day, she now gave way to a flood of tears. Her sister knelt beside her and comforted the little girl as best she could while Lord Waverly looked on from a discreet distance.

As Lady Sybil hovered above, watching this

scene, she could not help feeling a little disconcerted. She had cherished high hopes—and not without reason, she told herself—that Selinda and Waverly might by now have evinced some affection for each other. But they had entered the inn seemingly aloof and cold toward one another. Whatever could have happened? She knew quite well that nature had not bestowed more than a modicum of intelligence on her, but in matters of love she was never mistaken. These two were meant for each other and were, for some reason, fighting their attraction. Why must people in love always be so stupid? she wondered. As the party made their way up the stairs to Lucy's rooms, the ghost floated behind, puzzling over what must be done to set the matter right.

"It is a good thing," Lucy noted when they had shut the door, "that good Mrs. Bunche thinks that children eat as much as armies, for I believe there is enough for all of us."

As Lucy reported the events since their last meeting, they were able to make a satisfactory meal of steak soup, sliced ham, pigeon pie, iced cakes, cherry tartlet, and steamy chocolate, even though they were forced to share the same table service. "And so," Lucy concluded, "if that is not Rupert and Prudence in the town pillory, I am very much mistaken."

"It seems," said Lord Waverly after a thoughtful pause, "that all that remains to be done is to inform my man of business of this sudden turn of events."

"Oh, yes," Lucy said in matter-of-fact tones, "I

forgot to mention that I have already sent a short note off to Mr. Noon."

Selinda stared in no small dismay at her little sister. "How do you come to be acquainted with Lord Waverly's man of business?"

"Well, I'm not formally," Lucy told her, "but I did happen to remember his direction. What's more, he should have received his message before now, for that messenger left at the same time as the one I dispatched to you."

Now it was Selinda and Waverly's turn to explain that it had not been Lucy's note but a completely different collection of circumstances which had set them on her trail that morning.

"And so, I suppose my poor message waits all alone on some table or other for you to return, Lord Waverly," Lucy sighed, "only I pray you will burn it before you read it, for I would not have you guess how much a-tremble I was as I wrote it."

At this moment, Mrs. Bunche entered the room, still in her cloak and bonnet. She eyed Selinda and Lord Waverly with some glaring suspicion before Lucy assured her that these two were of a different cut of cloth than the last pair the good woman had encountered.

"Well, I hope so indeed, for I'll not countenance this poor child pulling squashed rats from the teeth of iron machines of the devil's invention! Howsomever, Miss Lucy," she went on before they could solicit an explanation of this odd declaration, "there is a gray, rabbity sort of gentleman waiting for you in the downstairs parlor who says you've sent for him."

"That, I suppose, would be Mr. Noon," Lucy ventured.

"From the description," Waverly told her, "I imagine you suppose correctly. Prepare yourself, ladies, to meet the most capable, competent, practical—and, therefore, terrifying—human on the face of the earth."

The little party found their way forthwith to a private parlor on the main floor. Mr. Noon was indeed a "rabbity sort of gentleman," just as Mrs. Bunche had informed them, and Lucy decided after she had looked him over that what he lacked in long ears he made up for in whiskers and twitches. So vivid was this image in her mind that she would swear ever afterward that she caught a glimpse of a white tuft from between his coattails.

Even though Lucy had explained only her own predicament (and that rather awkwardly, she supposed) in her hastily scrawled missive, Mr. Noon looked up unperturbed when the group entered the parlor. He had spread out in front of him what appeared to be a number of official documents and was giving instructions to an ancient clerk who was so bent as to resemble a question mark more than anything else.

"That will be all for the moment, Smythe," Mr. Noon told him with a brief twitch. "Good afternoon, my lord. I see you have arrived in a timely manner. Excellent. Quite excellent. Now we have several matters of business which must be attended to, but I assure you I shall ask for very little of your valuable time."

"I am at your disposal, Noon," his Lordship nodded.

"First, we have the matter of the miscreants. Basham, alias Shambeigh, was arrested in the early hours of this morning and has, I understand, given ready evidence against one Prudence Mordent, aliases too numerous to list, and her son, Rupert."

"They are now in the pillory in the village square," Lucy told him helpfully. Mr. Noon did not look up but merely leaned across to a list and, dipping his quill in ink, made a large checkmark next to an item.

"This quite naturally leaves Lady Selinda Harroweby and her sister, Lady Lucy Harroweby, without a legal guardian. Most distressing! Goes against the natural order of things! I have begun procedures to make them wards of the crown— which I think it wise they remain until each is twenty-five years of age. And so I have requested in my petition, my lord. We should have that matter completed within a fortnight. Then such guardians as the crown deems fit shall be appointed. In the meantime, I have arranged for a genteel lady of advanced years, Miss Hortensia Walleye, to serve as their companion and chaperon. She began her journey this morning and awaits you at Darrowdean," he said with a perfunctory nod to the girls.

At this announcement, Lucy and Selinda exchanged worried glances. "I beg your pardon, Mr. Noon," Selinda began. "My sister and I are most appreciative of your kind attention, you may be sure, but we have been sufficient company to one another for many years now."

"Yes," the gentleman returned dryly, "and we now see how effective that arrangement has been."

"Really, Noon," Lord Waverly protested, "is all this necessary?"

Mr. Noon paused a moment and twitched his whiskers before continuing in ironic tones, "I beg your Lordship will grant my superior, er, experience in matters of correctness. I have not yet met Miss Walleye, but I have been assured that she is *all* that is correct."

Lady Sybil, who had been pacing about in frustration, now froze in her tracks and shuddered. She could not recall when she had heard a more distressing pronouncement on a woman.

"Now, as to Darrowdean," Mr. Noon continued, pointedly oblivious to the consternation to which his arrangements had given rise, "all is much better than we had imagined. When I arrived, it appeared that the house had been entirely stripped of its contents, but most of these were found to be crated up in several of the outbuildings awaiting shipment to various auction houses. Miss Walleye will see to their unpacking and the reappointing of rooms."

"I see you have been very busy indeed, Noon," Lord Waverly smiled grimly.

Mr. Noon bowed. As he did so, he spotted the golden pomander hanging around Lucy's neck. "That, surely, is a family piece. Pray tell, just how did you come by it, Missy?"

Lucy gave him a highly abbreviated version of

the adventure in the coach, not mentioning, of course, the role Lady Sybil had played.

"Well, I see that it is quite damaged," Mr. Noon pronounced, pursing his lips into a thin, condescending smile. "Children are *not* ideal trustees of heirlooms, you will all agree. Now, give it here, child, and I shall see that it is repaired and deposited in my vault for the present."

At this, Lady Sybil cried out in extreme agitation. "You cannot allow it, Lucy! I vow, I shall not spend eternity in this man's wretched offices!"

This urgent complaint reminded Lucy rather forcibly of the gravity of Mr. Noon's suggestion, and she backed away from his outstretched hand, her face set in a threatening frown. "Come, come," Mr. Noon admonished as he approached her. "Recalcitrance is not attractive in a child. Miss Walleye will be shocked to see it in you. Now, then, give it here."

Lucy answered by retreating farther into a corner. "Come, Lucy," Lord Waverly intervened. "I shall take it and claim the honor of having it repaired for you. What's more," he continued in a low whisper, "I shall send it back direct to you when I have the chance."

Lucy glanced over at Lady Sybil. She was looking at Lord Waverly appraisingly. "It's all right, Lucy," she said after a moment. "I think Lord Waverly and I shall rub along famously."

As Lucy slowly handed the pomander to Lord Waverly, Mr. Noon broke in, "Very well, then, we must be on our way. I have a coach awaiting us outside, so we should arrive at Darrowdean before nightfall. I have bespoken rooms for you at The Golden Hour, my lord, unless you wish to return to London at once. *That* course I would strongly suggest, for you will allow that the propriety of this arrangement is questionable at best."

Lord Waverly did not, however, agree. A shadow of distress had shown itself in Selinda's eyes, he felt sure, at the mention of his leaving. It was a slim hope, but hope nonetheless.

Lucy, still on the lookout for Lady Sybil's best interests, cried out, "Oh, Lord Waverly, pray do not leave us so quickly. Please understand, Mr. Noon, we are all alone in the world. Do not give us over to complete strangers so quickly."

Mr. Noon wiggled his whiskers somewhat irritably by way of comment, but Lord Waverly knelt down beside the child and took her hand. "I shall send my coach back to London and ride alongside your coach. I shall not desert you, my dear." He looked up at Selinda then and for an instant caught what must have been a very warm expression. If only it had rested in her eyes longer before she withdrew behind her accustomed mask, he might have known for certain.

"We thank you very kindly for your escort, Lord Waverly," Selinda told him with downcast eyes.

"Come, come," Mr. Noon fussed. "We must make haste here. Miss Walleye awaits our arrival."

Mrs. Bunche hardly had time to summon herself to tears before her small guest climbed aboard Mr. Noon's carriage, but Lucy, sensitive to the woman's generous, tender nature, very kindly kissed her on the cheek and assured her that she would make The Laughing Lion a regular stop on her way to London whenever she passed that way.

"And when might that be?" the good woman asked, wiping away her tears.

Before Lucy could answer, Mr. Noon announced repressively that since the child would not make her London come-out for at least another eight years—children doing best, after all, in the country—he sincerely hoped Mrs. Bunche would continue in good health.

Mr. Noon climbed into the coach along with Selinda and Lucy. "I own I feel much relieved that our journey is underway at last," he told them as he consulted his timepiece. Considering that it had taken him no longer than fifteen minutes to dispatch his business at the inn, the sisters exchanged significant glances. Intercepting these darted looks, he frowned in deep disapproval and, after a moment, turned to Lucy and said, "Cover your ears, child. I would speak confidentially to your sister." Casting a sidelong glance at Selinda, Lucy complied with this command.

In spite of this precaution, Mr. Noon leaned forward and commenced to whisper. "Lord Waverly is my client and has been for years, and I would not for anything speak ill of him. But this is the very sort of scrape I have feared. He has a kind heart, as you have reason to know, and is said to be brilliant in such unprofitable studies as literature and philosophy. However, I must acknowledge he has not the least idea of the importance of conventions society has established for its security.

Had he not alerted me to your distress, I am afraid he would have compromised you so thoroughly that you would have been forced to wed and that is a connection we could on no account wish."

"I cannot think," Selinda began angrily, "that it is your business to meddle in the private life—"

"Tut, child, you cannot know your peril! You must realize that only Lord Waverly's fortune and family connections keep him from being cut entirely by the *ton*. I am sorry to say I long ago despaired of a proper connection for him. Although there is nothing precisely *objectionable* about your lines, my dear, I am afraid the precipitate actions you have taken in the last day or so bespeak a very intemperate and unschooled disposition. A very bad mix of blood, I am sorry to say. I cannot begin to think that the issue of such a union would bring anything but disgrace to both your names. Now do not frown so! Aside from my considerations for the House of Waverly, my integrity forces me to protect 'the orphan child' from the pitfalls that lie before her." He smiled briefly at what he fondly believed to be a witticism. "For you, my dear, Lord Waverly represents a pitfall from which your status in society would not recover. I do not think you can begin to imagine."

"Surely you are too nice, Mr. Noon," Selinda exclaimed hotly, deeply resenting his interference. "I cannot see that Lord Waverly's propensities, whatever they may be, can be as sinister as you represent them."

"Nothing sinister, my child, but everything singular. Do you know his country estate crawls with animals he has 'rescued,' as he calls it, from London and elsewhere? That he publicly cut a lady of unequaled reputation and standing merely because she had the good sense to disown her daughter who had found herself in, shall we say, an interesting condition? I do not think you can imagine how foolish the gentleman is."

"This sees to me like very good sense," Selinda said vehemently.

"I shudder to think of the education you have had if that is your opinion! I can see," he told her flatly, "that Miss Walleye's attentions will be essential."

Lucy, who had in fact heard every word with growing anger (for she had not covered her ears so very tightly), now felt obliged to save her sister from further distress. The coach was now passing through the village, and she called out for them to observe Prudence and Rupert being led away from the pillory. The guards, to all appearances, were having a difficult time of it. Now that Prudence's hands were free, she continued to make an attack on her son in spite of the efforts of the three or four burly keepers.

"I think they will do very well in the gaol for present," Mr. Noon told the girls. "I shall have to think whether it is best to petition their transportation or hanging."

Without hesitation, Lucy and Selinda cried out in horror, "Transportation!" and Mr. Noon's visage took on an appearance of severe affliction at this outburst.

Meanwhile, Lady Sybil rode along perched on

Lord Waverly's accommodating knee. She could not help but note the air of despondency which had settled over him since he embarked along the road. His silence was punctuated with an occasional sigh, and she could only wish that soliloquies were as common in life as they were on the stage. She, too, had taken note of Selinda's wistful glances in his direction and now she was certain that his heart was engaged as well. What sort of idiotic blindness could be afflicting the pair? she wondered.

It was well, she decided, that the pomander had fallen to his care rather than Lucy's, for, after all, it was the man who must speak. That must be it! The most common of all male idiocies! They always forgot to mention that they were in love! Well, tonight she would give him a dream which would make him act, or she was not Lady Sybil Harroweby.

# Chapter Twenty-one

When at last the carriage arrived at Darrowdean, it was well past dark. The high walls stood silhouetted against a cloudless moonlit night, and Lucy and Selinda knew that they were home at last. They were met at the familiar doors by Miss Hortensia Walleye who, thanks to Mr. Noon's glowing testimonials, had achieved legendary status. A few moments acquaintance, however, proved to Lucy that names are always significant. The woman clutched a branch of candles in one hand; the other held in their direction an enormous ear trumpet. Slowly, silently, she fixed the party with a baleful gaze, her pale, protruding eyes resolutely examining them one by one.

"Good evening," she shouted finally.

"Good evening, Miss Walleye—" Mr. Noon began.

"Eh?" she cried, swiveling the ear trumpet in his direction, barely missing him in the process.

"I said, 'good evening,'" he told her in a slightly louder voice.

"Mouth full of mush," the lady pronounced in what she must have assumed was an undertone.

"My name is Noon," he shouted. "Ezekiel Noon!"

"Aye," she bellowed back, "there's a full moon. What of it?"

"Noon!" he stormed, twitching furiously.

Lord Waverly and Lady Selinda each glanced in the direction of the flabbergasted Mr. Noon and, encountering each other's eyes, exchanged an amused look which threatened momentarily to bubble over into laughter. It was clearly the first time in many years that the man's painstaking plans had resulted in less than perfection. Now that he had caught Selinda's attention, Lord Waverly attempted to convey to her in his countenance the feelings he had been unable to put into words. She felt the warmth of his blazing eyes and remembered the way his lips had felt in her dream. Blushing suddenly, she looked away.

"Too late for gentlemen to call," Miss Walleye's voice blared. "Afternoon is for calls! Man as old as you should know that Mr. Noon!"

This pronouncement having been made, she took Selinda and Lucy by the shoulders and steered them uncompromisingly through the door. Mr. Noon, atwitch indeed, backed out of the door onto the walk, taking Waverly with him. The door closed resoundingly on the pair without further ceremony.

"Men!" Miss Walleye roared. "No more sense than monkeys. A good deal less. To bed now. We'll have some talk in the morning."

The lady turned then without further ado and led Selinda and Lucy up the wide central staircase. They had been looking about at the hall ever since their entry, noting uneasily the changes since their last visit. Furniture had been set about and paintings hung on every wall, but nothing was where it ought to be. In spite of the amusement offered by their deaf companion, it was, all in all, a cold, dispiriting homecoming. It had been a long day, however, and both of them looked forward to the comfort of their chambers, perhaps a few moments of conversation (which Mr. Noon's presence in the coach constrained), and the bliss of sleep.

"I am much afraid," Miss Walleye told them loudly, "that such servants as I could engage on so short notice have only readied the one chamber, for we expected only Lady Lucy. You two must share for tonight and tomorrow we shall do better.

"In the morning," she went on, "I shall begin to work with you, Lady Selinda. From what Noon has written me, I imagine you were most shockingly unready for your London come-out. I have dispatched an advertisement for a governess for Lady Lucy, but it is my hope that my cousin, Miss Mehitabelle Walleye, will be able to undertake that position. She is a trifle advanced in years and only has one good eye, but she formed the pattern for my early years and I do not think that one could ask for more." With these resonant words still echoing in the passage, she bid them good night and made her lumbering way to a chamber just across the hall.

Some good angel, Lucy decided, had prompted Miss Walleye to select their old chamber for them, for she and Selinda had always shared a room. The furnishings were different, but the proper draperies and counterpane had been chosen, so the room looked quite its old self, and this was comforting. A fire blazed on the grate, and its glow cast a rosy, welcoming light. In spite of appearances and pronouncements, they could not be insensible to the fact that Miss Walleye's management was a good deal less distressing than the oppressive economies of their supposed Aunt Prudence.

Selinda threw herself down on the bed and sighed. The image of Lord Waverly's expression when last she encountered it was etched in her memory. She could swear he loved her, but still, he had never spoken. Were all men so provoking, she wondered? In the books she read, gentlemen had made their pronouncements of love in spite of worse opposition than she and Lord Waverly faced. Surely, she told herself, Lord Waverly was not so much in the thrall of Mr. Noon that he could not love where he wished. Oh! Nothing made sense. If love were this painful, she wanted nothing of it.

Lucy crawled up beside her on the bed and sighed, too. "Enough adventures for you, Selinda?" "Yes," Selinda frowned, "and all of the wrong kind. Life does not seem to have much in common with our lovely novels, Lucy. That much I have learned. I begin to fear I must learn to keep a rational head on my shoulders and mind what Miss Walleye says, however tedious it seems."

"You cannot mean it, Selinda!" Lucy cried in distress. "Not any of it! It is too dreadful."

"So is disappointment, Lucy," she said with a catch in her throat.


The Golden Hour was every bit as comfortable an establishment as The Laughing Lion, Lord Waverly was glad to discover, for he felt that, even if a warm fire and a bottle of brandy might not solve his dilemma, they might go a fair distance to dull his distress. He had wondered the whole length of the journey whether he was setting himself a fool's errand by pursuing Lady Selinda's heart. Sometimes he would stake his whole fortune that her heart was engaged. Then he would be just as certain he had imagined it. It was true, he told himself, that circumstances had contrived to make his courtship the most botched-up thing imaginable. He knew quite well that the usual flowers and verses would not do for Lady Selinda, yet stolen kisses in church combined with a precipitous cross-country flight hardly seemed the thing either.

He poured a second glass of brandy and stared into the fire, wondering what to do. On the way to the inn, Mr. Noon had informed him of the regimen he had mapped out for Lady Selinda. It was clear from the man's repressive tone that he did not think it suitable for his Lordship to pay the lady any further attention. In fact, the stern old man had all but read Waverly a lecture on propriety. If he knew anything about Mr. Noon, and Lord Waverly fancied he did, access to Selinda would be the main obstacle to the advancement of his courtship. He toyed briefly with the notion of merely dismissing the man, but Mr. Noon and his father before him had managed the affairs of the House of Waverly and it simply would not do. He knew he had to act quickly to engage the lady's heart, but how? He must find a way to circumvent Noon's interference. If only life were as simple as in books, he mused as his eyes grew heavy.

Lady Sybil had been watching Lord Waverly meditatively for some minutes. As usual, she waited until she was quite sure he was deeply asleep—half an hour was usually sufficient—before she allowed herself to enter his dream. When she did, she smiled broadly and wondered if her attentions were necessary after all. But, still, what harm could there be to add a few details?

It was a warm, starry night in Lord Waverly's dream. Fragrant roses twined up a picturesque balcony. Leaning over the edge, a fair maiden with eloquent green eyes and soft brown ringlets was sighing into the darkness. By the light of an enormous moon, Lord Waverly could see a tear tracing its way down her cheek. He moved closer. Her lips trembled as she spoke one word, "Waverly." His heart pounded.

In the velvety moonlight, he climbed with extraordinary ease up to the balcony and whispered in return, "I am here, my love," She turned and stepped to him, melting into his arms. He

245

could feel the warm softness of her body through her gossamer robe and traced with his hands her narrow waist and the curving swell of her hips. Eagerly, she pulled his mouth to hers. It tasted of roses, he thought unaccountably.

"If you had not come, Roland, I must surely have died of sadness," she told him after a moment. "I have waited so long for you to speak. You know that a lady must not speak of these things or by any action imply that . . . that her heart is irretrievably engaged."

So that was it, he thought sleepily. It was as simple as that.


Waverly pulled himself from his dream with a sudden start. It really was that simple—or could be. If Selinda's heart were engaged, she could surely not display any evidence of it. He had forgotten entirely about that. What a sapskull he was to overlook the oppressive role convention played in love. Rising quietly he peered out into the hall. A light still shone from under Mr. Noon's door and the sound of a quill being dragged inexorably across vellum echoed in the darkness. He slung a cloak over his shoulders, and, pulling off his boots, he tiptoed like a schoolboy down the corridor. Behind him, Lady Sybil floated along, sending desperate thoughts to Lucy to aid in this night's endeavor.


Lucy and Selinda sat quietly by the fire. Lucy's

thoughts had been strangely beset all evening with odd visions of her sister and Lord Waverly. She knew as surely as anything that they were in love and that there was something she must do to promote their courtship. She felt a sharp tugging at her heart that whatever it was must be done tonight. But what on earth could it be?

Idly, she paced the room. She was not yet tired enough to go to bed, for she had slept late that day. Then she spotted a prayer book by Selinda's reticule. How odd! She opened it, read a page, and smiled as she remembered her sister's subterfuge. Fair Rosamonde's adventures were certainly out of place between such pious covers. As she turned the pages slowly, a light dawned in her eyes, and she knew what she must do.

Lucy waited perhaps a half an hour longer, for she did not want to inconvenience her sister for long, and Lord Waverly, she knew, needed some time to make preparations. She only hoped that she was not mistaken in her intuition this time.

"Selinda," she said at last in a tremulous voice.

"What is it, Lucy?" her sister asked kindly.

Lucy swallowed her guilt. "I have an odd notion that someone is on the grounds. You do not suppose that Prudence and Rupert could have escaped and come to get me?"

Selinda looked at her sister's wide-eyed expression. Poor little thing, she thought sadly. With all that she had been through it was not to be wondered at if she took strange frights. "I do not think they can have," Selinda smiled reassuringly.

"I am very frightened," Lucy said in an even smaller voice.

Selinda came over to her and took her in her arms and patted her reassuringly. "I do not think you need fear anyone ever again."

Lucy bit her lip. It went against her grain, but it must be done. "I am so *very* frightened, Selinda. You must look out and make certain that they have not climbed up onto the balcony."

Selinda shook her head and laughed gently. "Those great fat things? Why the balcony would fall and crush them both."

Lucy pulled out her lower lip and allowed two great tears to well up in her eyes.

Selinda sighed. "Oh, very well, Lucy, if it will make you feel better."

Opening the French doors, Selinda stepped out onto the balcony and even made a show of leaning out to take a better look. "You see now, Lucy . . ." she was saying, just as she heard the doors latch behind her.

Lord Waverly had saddled the horse himself rather than wait for a groom and had sped through the night as if the devil himself were behind him. He would have been extremely interested to know that particular post, directly in back of him on the saddle, was occupied by the great-great grandmother of the woman he loved.

It was not far from the inn to Darrowdean, still the ride seemed to last at least a lifetime. His resolve faltered slightly as he recollected how untoward his actions would seem; however, he told himself, if she loved him, it would work. If she didn't, nothing would. In for a penny, in for a pound.

There was only one lighted window at Darrowdean and Waverly rode toward it. He could only pray that he would find Selinda rather than that quiz, Miss Walleye. Even so, he told himself resolutely, he would try each of the hundred odd windows until dawn if he had to.

He dismounted and led his mount in the direction of the light. The room was on the second story and appeared to have a balcony. His heart began to race. He had not ever believed in dreams before, but he was beginning to now, for miraculously it appeared that someone was on the balcony pacing. As he came closer, he could see that it was indeed Selinda.

There were no roses, but a sturdy vine, thankfully without thorns, twined its way upward, and Lord Waverly was easily able to climb it. He swung himself quietly onto the balcony where Selinda now stood with her back toward him, chafing her arms and shivering.

"Lady Selinda . . ." he whispered.

She turned abruptly and threw herself into his arms. He sat back on the edge of the balcony, taking her onto his lap and wrapping his cloak about her.

"Waverly," she shivered, "I am so glad you are here. I fear I should have died—"

It was a very fortunate thing that he chose just then to cover her lips with his own before she had a chance to continue with ... *of the cold for that dratted Lucy has taken it into her head to lock me out.* It was fortunate, too, that a moment later his words were, "I love you to distraction, Selinda. I cannot live without you. You must say you will be my wife."

By way of answer, Selinda snuggled closer, kissed him quite soundly, and sighed, "I am so glad you are finally decided on it, my love. Otherwise I should have had to have ridden out and abducted you, and I am sure that tedious Mr. Noon would have tried to read me a lecture!"

Lady Sybil, who had watched this very gratifying scene with ghostly tears pricking at her eyes, now floated through the wall into the chamber where Lucy, too, had been observing the results of her maneuvering.

"Good evening, Lucy," the ghost said.

"Hello, Lady Sybil," she whispered in return.

"I have been sending you mental messages this last hour or so. I am glad to see they have been effective."

"I wondered why my thoughts were so tingly. I should have guessed it was you. But, I say, how do you come to be here? Ought you not to be in Lord Waverly's pocket?"

The ghost's silvery laughter tinkled at this naive error of speech. "Darrowdean was my bridal settlement," she told Lucy. "I can stay with you here as long as I like."

"Capital," cried Lucy.

"And if Miss Walleye does not suit, I fear the place will agree with her very little."

250

Lucy smiled mischievously and turned her attention back to the window. Selinda's arms were wrapped around Lord Waverly's neck as he climbed over the edge of the balcony. In a few moments, they could hear the hoofbeats echoing away into the darkness.

"It is a good thing Selinda was furious with me or she would never have left."

"A very good thing indeed," the ghost concurred.

# Epilogue

The full blazing sun of the tropical sky beat down on Prudence Mordent. It had been almost six months since the ship that was to have transported them to the penal colony in Australia sank and she and Rupert had floated to this island on the same broad plank.

"Faster," she snapped irritably at a small boy who immediately commenced to swing the palm frond more vigorously about her head. It was not always easy to make herself understood, but such petty irritations aside, she was content with her life here. Strangely, the inhabitants of this island paradise had accepted her punishing presence and tyrannical commands unquestioningly. Unbeknownst to her, mere days before she and her son washed up on the beach, a bad-tempered witch doctor had prophesied that the gods were about to inflict a punishment greater than the usual typhoon. The scowl on Prudence's unlovely face demonstrated at once to the chastened populace that the gods were angry, indeed, and the frightened masses had fallen at once to their knees.

Beneath the waving palm frond, Prudence scrutinized the activity in front of her. A royal palace was being built for her, albeit of bamboo; busy workers were also gathering fruit for the distillery. Essentials, then, were being attended to. In the distance she could see a perspiring Rupert balancing a heavy load on his head while an enormous woman flung invectives at him in the native tongue. Yes, she had chosen a good bride for him, she thought with a grim smile. Nothing like a tyrannical wife to help a son to appreciate his mother.

Oblivious to dark whisperings of rebellion about her, she called loudly for another plate of breadfruit.

When the same sun passed the meridian and made its way over England, it eventually shone down on a lively party driving through the shaded lanes of Hyde Park. Selinda and Waverly still sat hand in hand, oblivious to the distress of onlookers who shuddered at the sight of a man so very much in love with his wife. The other side of the carriage was occupied by Lucy and the invisible Lady Sybil Harroweby. Neither, it turned out, had been destined to stay long in the countryside. On returning from their elopement to Paris, Selinda and Waverly had swooped down on Darrowdean with armloads of presents and very little censure for Lucy's unaccountable behavior that night a few weeks earlier.

As Lady Sybil had predicted, Darrowdean had proved extremely disagreeable to Miss Walleye. As soon as Selinda's absence was discovered, reported, and condemned, the lady had turned her attentions assiduously to poor Lucy. The miserable child practiced curtseys, painted screens, netted purses, and walked about with books on her head until she was ready to scream. The last straw came when Miss Walleye consigned Lucy's hoard of romantic novels to the drawing-room fire and prescribed a rigid program of improving readings for the child. Enough was quite enough. Later in the week, the lady had suddenly fled without giving notice after a series of inexplicably upsetting dreams. Somehow, in all the fuss, no one remembered to inform Mr. Noon and Lucy was thus able to order her life as she pleased until her sister's return.

As the carriage rounded a curve, Lucy cried out, "Look over there, Selinda. Can that lady possibly be Miss Snypish?"

"I believe it is," Selinda agreed slowly on examining the pair seated on a bench beneath a flowering linden tree. "And the gentleman? Can that possibly be your cousin, my dear?"

"By heavens, it is Bastion!" Waverly exclaimed, his conscience suddenly a bit ruffled. "I must say, I do feel a little guilty about the trick I played him."

Commanding his driver to pull aside, the party stepped down and approached the odd couple before them. Miss Snypish, or the Marchioness of Bastion as she was now known, rose up at once and twisted her face into an odd grimace intended as a smile. That expression was still not easy for her to achieve, but it was immediately clear she had been working at it.

As they drew closer, Lucy and Selinda realized they had never seen such a change in a woman before. She looked now quite plump, and, although her features were every bit as sharp, her glance was not nearly so intimidating as it once had been.

After diffident greetings had been exchanged, Lord Waverly took his cousin aside a bit while the ladies chatted with all appearance of amiability.

"I must apologize, Bastion," Lord Waverly began fervently. "You must believe I never meant for it to come to this."

"Not a word, Waverly," Bastion told him firmly. He paused a moment and then went on with solemn dignity, "I do not know what I should have done without Letitia. I was past praying for, as you have cause to know, till she took me in hand. You would not know me, Waverly."

Waverly looked doubtfully at his cousin. "If you should need anything, Cousin . . . money . . ."

Bastion made a curt gesture of annoyance. "You do not understand, Waverly. She has remade me completely. I was bitter at first, but now . . ." He broke off suddenly and looked back at his wife. "She's a remarkable woman, Waverly. A woman of talent and . . . passion!"

255

* * *

Later in the coach, Waverly told Selinda, "It is an odd ending, I'll be bound. Odder than any book!"

Selinda laughed and took his arm, "Nay, sir. Better than any book!"